THE SENSITIVES

BOOK ONE

RICK WOOD

BLOOD SPLATTER PRESS

YOU NEVER EXPECT A SWEET, DARLING LITTLE GIRL TO BE THE source of a man's deepest fear.

Yet all Detective Inspector Jason Lyle could get from his colleague was gibberish. Eccentrically formed, incoherent, insubstantial gibberish.

"She – she – her eyes... her eyes..."

"For Christ's sake, pull yourself together," Jason demanded, rolling his eyes and folding his arms.

"You don't know," retorted the constable. "You weren't there..." He threw his arms around his body, shaking in a frenzied huddle, his bloodshot eyes staring wide-eyed at a vacant corner of the room.

With an exasperated sigh, Jason nodded at the nearest officer and the constable was led away, leaving Jason alone in his office.

Sitting back in his grand, leather office chair, he picked up a mug and sniffed it. It smelt like coffee. He needed coffee.

He took a sip.

He almost retched as he spat it back out. He hated cold coffee. It was all he ever seemed to find around his office –

cold bloody coffee. Where was that constable who said he was bringing Jason a decent, hot cup of coffee?

Probably blubbering with the other pathetic excuse for a police officer, he thought to himself, shaking his head. *Is that what passes the training nowadays?*

Jason cast his wizened, cynical eyes upon a photo frame at the edge of his desk. His wife and his daughter stood, proudly smiling back at him, and he considered his sweet daughter's face. Nine years old, the same age as the girl who had mortified his officer into a blubbering mess. His daughter's face was so innocent, full of such impenetrable virtue. How could a girl, like his daughter, ever be considered as volatile as they were making this witness out to be?

"Fuck it," he coughed, springing out of his chair and dropping the remnants of his stale coffee mug into a full wastepaper basket leant haphazardly against his desk.

If this girl was really that bad, he was going to have to see it for himself. If an officer couldn't take a simple statement from a child without turning into a pathetic wreck, then it would be up to him to take the responsibility.

Bloody amateurs.

He threw off his jacket, loosened his collar, and rolled up his sleeves as he trooped toward the interrogation room. People tried to say hello as he passed, but he ignored every one of them. He didn't need pointless, going-nowhere conversations – once he had tunnel vision, he didn't care about the chitchat some boring idiot wanted to start with him.

He reached the interrogation room, turned the handle, and was taken aback to find it locked. He shuffled the handle again, checking he wasn't mistaken.

"Oi!" he shouted, expecting someone to hear and come to his beck and call.

As he had hoped, Gus pointed his head out of a nearby kitchen, pieces of yumyum hanging off his fat cheek.

"What's up, Jason?" Gus inquired, his overweight belly sickening Jason at the sight of what constitutes a police officer nowadays.

"Why the bloody hell is that door locked?" Jason commanded.

"That's where we're keeping that Kaylee Kemple girl, boss," Gus replied dumbly, staring back with thick, inquisitive eyes.

"Yes, I know that," Jason spat through seething teeth. "Why is it locked?"

"Have you met her?"

"No, I have not."

"Then you wouldn't understand."

Jason did all he could to contain his rage. His fists clenched, his fingers flexed, his eyes narrowed. His chest throbbed with his accelerating heartbeat and he found his body unconsciously leaning aggressively toward Gus.

"What the fuck wouldn't I understand?" Jason spoke in a hostile but quiet voice – trying adamantly to remain professional and contain his incessant fury. "It is a little girl. What the hell is wrong with you people?"

"Honestly, Inspector, you haven't met her."

"Well then open the door, I would like to."

Despite the obvious intensity of Jason's anger, the throbbing veins on his perspiring forehead, and the bloodshot fever of his eyes – Gus wobbled.

Gus did not want to endure Jason's wrath; no one did. Jason's anger was legendary. But at the same time, he did not want to have to face what was behind that door.

"Gus," Jason began again, slowly, furiously. "I'm going to ask you one final time. Open. The fucking. Door."

Gus' arms shook, his whole body seizing in fear. Taking the keys off his belt, he presented them to Jason, who took them reluctantly.

"Here," Gus offered. "Take them. But please wait for me to go back in the kitchen."

Gus scuttled away like a pathetic little beetle, slamming the kitchen door behind him.

"Fucking charlatan," Jason muttered, placing the key in the lock.

He had barely reached the first rotation of the key before he froze. A murmur reverberated against the door, vibrating with a croaky breath. A low-pitched rumble that sounded like the deep laughter of an old, demented man echoed from within.

Was that the girl?

Fuck's sake, Jason, don't let it go to your head. It's a nine-year-old.

Ignoring his instinct, he turned the key and opened the door, entering the room and shutting himself in.

He regretted his lack of trepidation instantly. His whole body shuddered. His breath was visible in the air – it was the middle of summer, but this room was like the Antarctic.

Two blond pigtails outlined the head of the girl. She sat completely stationary, facing the opposite wall, humming a quietly chaotic low-pitched tune – a repetitive, incessant tune-less song. Jason didn't know why, but this song sent chills firing up and down his spine.

"Kaylee, my name is Detective Inspector Jack Lyle," he introduced himself. "Mind if I speak to you?"

The humming ended.

Intense, unbearable silence screamed from the back of the girl's head.

"I'm sorry, Kaylee's not here right now," she answered. "Can I take a message?"

TEWKESBURY. THE PLACE THAT ALWAYS FLOODED, WAS FULL OF old people, and where everyone knew everyone else.

Except for Oscar.

No one knew Oscar. Except for his mum, his dad, and his cat.

And, very briefly, those people he served on the checkout in Morrison's, though his interaction with these strangers was usually short, often involving a grunt for a greeting and a snarl for goodbye.

Oscar hated working on the checkouts, but he couldn't be arsed to stay in school. He had counted down the weeks until the end of year eleven when he could leave; meaning no more work, no more homework, and no more having to deal with annoying teachers. He could just sit around on his arse all day doing nothing. It was a dream come true.

Then he reached eighteen, and his parents charged him rent.

This was where he ended up. Stuck behind the checkout in Morrison's. With eight hours to go. And a lot of customers that he had to pretend to care about.

"Murgh," grunted a man as he placed his Stella Artois on the belt, handed Oscar a crumpled five-pound note, and plodded back to his miserable life.

However miserable the man's life was, Oscar envied it. The guy had a four-pack of beer and didn't need to sit there serving miserable farts for the next seven hours fifty-eight minutes.

Oscar was aware that he didn't have the kind, welcoming face that would encourage someone to engage in conversation with him. And if someone did try to engage him in conversation, he would find it the most tedious few minutes of his day. He really hated small talk; any acknowledgement of another human beyond a "murgh" was immensely tedious. A fully formed "hello" was the extreme limit of the interaction he was comfortable with.

Yet, some people still tried. Why? Why couldn't they just go through their life leaving him the hell alone?

Oscar was a thin, scrawny young man. Lazy and unmotivated, but too lazy to really care that he was unmotivated. He spent most of his time between being moaned at by his parents for doing nothing with his life, playing FIFA, being moaned at by his parents for not washing up, going to counselling, collecting his anxiety medication, being moaned at by his parents for not caring about the fact he was having to take anxiety medication, then being moaned at that he's not caring about the fact that he's being moaned at.

Maybe that's why I'm so lazy. I've numbed my brain with pills.

His parents would claim it was his Xbox that deadened him – but it was the pills.

Or it could be his Xbox.

Who gives a shit, really?

"Hello, dearie," smiled an old lady as she placed a bunch of bananas, some paracetamol, and a jar of coffee on the belt. Before Oscar could get too irritated by the fact that this old lady had forced two fully formed two-syllable words upon him, he noticed her placing her debit card into the machine and entering her pin number before Oscar had even scanned her items.

"No, you've got to wait," Oscar told her.

"What's that, dear?"

"I need to put your things through first."

"Yes, you put them through, dear."

"Now you need to enter your pin."

"I need to do what?"

"Enter your pin."

"But I already have."

"No, you need to enter it again."

"But then you'd charge me twice!"

Fuuuuuuuuuuuuuuucking heeeeeeeeeeeeeell.

"No. It did not go through because it wasn't ready. I need you to do it now."

"Oh, okay then."

"Yes, I need you to do it now."

"Oh, is it ready now?"

"Yes, it is ready."

"Are you sure? Because I've already done it once."

"Please put your pin in."

I'm going to shoot myself.

"Now you need to press enter."

"Do what, dear?"

"Press enter."

"Oh, where's that?"

"In the bottom right."

"Okay."

"No, that's the clear button, you've just cleared it. Now you need to enter your pin again."

"What's that?"

"You need to enter your pin again."

"But I've already done it twice."

Aaaaaaaaaaarrrrrrrgggggghhhhhhhh!!

"Tell you what; why don't we just use contactless?"

He grabbed the woman's card, held it against the machine, and handed it back to her, beaming a huge fake smile toward her confused face.

Seven hours fifty-six minutes to go.

Oscar sat back in his chair – a plastic chair falling to pieces and digging into his back, which was surely against union regulations – if there was a union for dead-end supermarket workers, that is.

He ran his hands through his greasy, unkempt hair.

Was this what his life had in store for him?

Eighteen years old. He was supposed to be in the prime of his life.

Across the supermarket, some guy with a lip piercing, shorts, and a woolly hat on, put his arms around his girlfriend. His girlfriend was stunning – long, blond hair, curvy waist, succulent arse. Oscar couldn't help but stare – but mostly at the guy. Why on earth had a woman like this chosen a man like that?

I mean, the guy was wearing shorts *and* a woolly hat. Which one is it? Was it hot or cold?

Unsure why it was making him angry, he found his arms shaking and his legs wobbling. This bloke infuriated him. Not just because he dressed like an inept idiot – but because he had managed to bag himself a gorgeous girl.

No girl ever looked Oscar's way.

Ever.

The more and more he glared at this man, the more he felt his anger raging, intensifying, multiplying, as the man packed his cereal, his condoms, and his Coke, picking his plastic bag up in his hand and taking it away and – *BANG!*

The man fell to the floor, a bloody hole sent straight

through his body, falling to his knees, clutching his chest. His girlfriend wept over him, desperately clinging onto him, screaming for dear life.

Oscar glanced over his shoulder to see if anyone else was reacting, and looked back, then–

They were fine.

The guy and his girlfriend were absolutely fine.

Everyone carried on like nothing had happened.

What the hell?

The guy placed his sleazy arm around his girlfriend's shoulders, giving her a disgusting open-mouth kiss that looked like he was a frog trying to eat a tadpole.

But he was alive. Perfectly well.

No one else reacted. No one else had seen anything.

Oscar clambered into his pocket for his anxiety medication. He withdrew it, popping out four pills, shoving them in his mouth and swallowing without the need for water.

"Oi, mate, pay attention!"

Oscar's head shot around. An irritable old man was waiting for his shopping to be scanned.

Willing his heavy breathing to subside and his alert mind to calm down, Oscar picked up a loaf of bread and beeped it through.

It was just his overactive imagination.

This was why he took the pills.

Seven hours fifty-two minutes to go.

3

"We were... reluctant" – began the well-dressed lawyer, pulling a face as if he was chewing something disgusting – "to hire you. I mean, what you do... I don't, particularly, believe in it."

April sighed, chewing her gum with an open mouth just to irritate this toffy, privately educated, stuck-up-his-own-arse, insufferable man. Sure, April liked to dye her hair purple. Sure, she had more tattoos and piercings than this man was comfortable with. And sure, she worked in the paranormal investigating business, something perhaps not given much integrity by the educated elite – it didn't mean this pompous arse got to talk to her so condescendingly.

"But, our client," the lawyer continued, "he, er... he insisted on it. If it were up to me–"

"Looks like it ain't up to you, though, don't it?" April responded, forcing a smarmy, insincere smile to her lips. Yes, it was childish to stoop to his level of condescension – but it felt good to get one over on him.

"We're aren't particularly interested in your opinion, I'm

afraid," Julian pointed out, so stern and diplomatic. "Where is Henry?"

"Just through those doors."

"Lovely," Julian confirmed. "Thank you."

Julian made his way through the double doors first, followed by April – who made sure to give the lawyer a huge, fury-provoking grin.

"What a prick," April observed as she and Julian walked toward the bench where their client sat.

"You need to stay more detached, April," Julian replied. "I know the guy's a prick, but we still need to be professional."

As they approached Henry, April was taken aback by how normal he looked. Despite his hands being in handcuffs and being adorned in prison wear, he looked like the average father. A mixture of brown and grey hair, stubble on his chin, and a sensitive frown on his kind face. Henry looked wounded, as if the events were distressing him immensely – something April had no doubt they were.

"Mr Kemple, it's good to meet you," Julian greeted him, always professional.

"Thank you," Henry replied, raising from his seat in respect. "I would shake your hand, but it's a little difficult."

"Not to worry." Julian smiled as they sat down, April taking a seat beside Julian.

"And please, call me Henry."

April couldn't help but admire how good Julian was with people. He was a gifted exorcist and an accomplished demonologist, there was no doubt about that. And the way he'd taken her off the street when she was younger and taught her to hone her powers, moulding her into the strong, nineteen-year-old woman she had become, was nothing short of heroic. He had a natural air of confidence about him that didn't come off as smug, but as warm and inviting. Perhaps this came from him being almost ten years older than she, and maybe April would learn that patience in time.

"My name is Julian, and this is April. The first question is probably the most obvious one, but I'll ask it anyway," began Julian. "How are you, Henry?"

"Well…" Henry shook his head, looking to his feet. He fought off tears, his face scrunching as he visibly willed himself not to break. "Not good."

"Yes, I can imagine. It's pretty horrific circumstances."

"I just… I can't believe I'm here."

"I imagine it must be devastating."

Henry forced an absent nod as he wiped his eyes on his sleeve.

"Why don't you start from the beginning, Henry?"

"My daughter, Kaylee… She's only nine-years-old. We've always been so close, best friends, even. I took her to parks, zoos, did everything a good dad does. Then one day, she just…"

He trailed off again, forcing tears away.

"Take your time," Julian reassured him.

"She just changed. Became nothing short of sadistic. Started doing all these nasty things."

"When did she start doing these things?"

"Three, four months ago."

"And what kind of things did she do?"

Henry stared back at Julian, his eyes widening, his lips pursed together. His body shook. He visibly willed his lip to stop quivering.

"Horrific things," Henry gasped.

"What kind of horrific things, Henry?"

"She stole the razors from my shaver and cut my wife's arms whilst she was sleeping. I woke up and she was unconscious; I had to rush her to the hospital. Kaylee denied it was her, but I knew. She had this, this far-off look in her eyes, like a distant evil. It was a look I'd never seen before."

"Sounds awful."

"She would spy on me and my wife when we made love. We'd do it after she'd gone to bed, of course, check she was fast asleep, be silent – but the door would be open. We'd hear her breathing. When I'd approach she'd run away, then I'd find her asleep in her room. Then, there was the time…"

"Yes?"

"She sawed our cat's leg off. She got a…"

Henry's eyes gave in and he waved his hand to indicate no more. He turned his face away, covering himself with his arm.

"Sorry," Henry muttered.

"It's quite all right," Julian reassured him. "So why are you here? Why were you arrested?"

"She… She told everyone I molested her. She told everyone I touched her!" His face broke, and his whole body convulsed in tears. "How could I? She's my daughter! I'm a doctor, for Christ's sake! I would never touch her, I wouldn't. I love her! I love her so much."

Julian glanced at April, who had remained an intrigued voyeur for the duration of the interview. His eyes indicated it was time to go.

"What we will do, Henry," Julian began, resting a comforting hand on Henry's shoulder. "We will talk to Kaylee. We will see what we make of her, and let you know what our verdict is."

Henry managed to force a nod, but couldn't get out any words between his furious sobbing.

With a nod to April, Julian stood and led them out. They remained silent until they left the police station.

"So," April declared, breaking the silence. "What did you make of him?"

"Either he's a very good liar, or we have a deranged child on our hands."

Julian stared into the distance, distracted by something, his eyes glazing over.

"What is it?" April prompted.

"I can feel something," Julian replied. "There's someone near. A new Sensitive. Someone who's just starting to discover his gift. I can feel it."

April watched Julian, peering at the troubled look taking him over.

"How do you know?"

"Because it feels the same as when I found you."

April nodded. Julian was normally spot on about these things.

"What do we do?"

Julian took a deep intake of breath, held it, and let it go.

"Find him," Julian confirmed. "Before his powers get the better of him... and someone gets hurt."

4

THERE WAS NO WAY TO SIT IN A COUNSELLING SESSION WITHOUT being uncomfortable, or so Oscar decided. He could lay down on the sofa like he'd seen people do in the movies, but that just felt weird. He could sit forward intently, but that would be too intense. As it was, he decided to shift between sitting back and sitting on the edge of his chair, never quite able to get comfortable.

"Tell me about your week," Doctor Jane Middlemore requested, preparing her pen and her pad and peering over her glasses at Oscar.

Oscar shifted again, placing his hands over his lap, covering a poorly timed erection. How could a counsellor be so attractive? Oscar could barely concentrate. She had long, red hair, prominent bosoms, and wore a fitted suit, with a slit in her skirt that traipsed all the way up to her thigh. Oscar knew he was staring at her thigh, and he needed to stop, as it was becoming painfully obvious.

He couldn't help it. Her skin was impeccably smooth, and her thigh was perfectly rounded.

Damn it. I'm being such a perv. Stop it.

"My week's been okay."

"And how are you feeling?"

Horny.

"Tired, mostly."

"How come?"

Oscar sighed.

Who cares?

I mean, honestly, what difference is confiding in this ridiculously hot woman going to make about anything? Is it going to make him feel better? Change who he is? Make him less of an unmotivated arse?

Honestly, the only thing Oscar cared about was going home and playing FIFA.

"Oh, you know. Playing on my Xbox too much."

Then the most peculiar thing happened.

Out of the corner of his eye, Oscar was sure he could see a masculine figure. Someone standing behind Jane with a relaxed, cocky demeanour.

But as soon as Oscar turned his gaze toward the figure, it went. Like a puff of smoke immediately dispersing.

"What about a girlfriend? Have you thought about going out and meeting someone, perhaps instead of sitting alone playing with your Xbox?"

"I'd love to meet someone, except I don't really think anyone would love to meet me."

The cocky strut of some laddish bloke walked past in the reflection of a window. Jane didn't react.

How could she not see him?

He shot his head around to glance at whoever it was, but it was gone. Nothing. Just a passing hallucination out of the corner of his eyes.

Now I'm seeing things? I'm all kinds of messed up...

"And why is it you think no one would like to meet you?"

"I don't know, it's just–"

And just at that moment, as if appearing from nothing, evolving into a fully formed body, appeared a bloke. Standing at Jane's side. Shaved head, pierced eyebrow, and baggy tracksuit hanging off a well-sculpted bare chest.

Oscar's jaw hung wide open. He blinked his eyes tightly a few times, as if the man would go away as soon as he averted his gaze. But the mirage was still there, standing prominently in the flesh.

Jane glanced over her shoulder, then back to Oscar, trying to find the subject of her gaze, but seeing nothing.

How is she not seeing this?

"Honestly, Jane," the guy grunted. "You're doin' ma fuckin' 'ead in. It's like you're more obsessed with your job. I may as well move my shit out."

Oscar's mind was awash with confusion. He stared dumbfoundedly at this miraculously appeared man, spewing abuse at his counsellor.

"What is going on?" Oscar demanded.

"What do you mean?" Jane replied, completely undeterred by the man beside her.

"What is your boyfriend doing here?"

Oscar closed his eyes and shuddered. When he opened his eyes, the man was gone. Completely disappeared, as if he was never there.

But he had been there.

Oscar was certain of it.

Despite Jane furiously looking over her shoulder to the space Oscar had just shouted at, despite her seeing nothing – he had been there. Oscar had seen him.

"Excuse me?"

"With his skinhead, tracksuit, abs, eyebrow piercing. He was there."

"How on earth do you know what my boyfriend looks like? Have you been spying on me?"

"He wanted to know why you're too busy with your job, and whether he should move out."

Jane's jaw dropped. For a few moments she stared at Oscar in bewildered shock, her eyebrows raised, her body stiffened.

Then her body changed. Her eyebrows narrowed, her fists clenched, and she stood suddenly, jabbing her finger toward the door.

"I think you need to leave!" Jane demanded. "And if you come near me or my boyfriend again, I will call the police!"

Oscar froze.

But he had been there! Oscar had seen him. As clear as he saw Jane at that moment, pointing a vehemently shaking arm toward the door.

"Go!" she shouted once more.

Oscar jumped to his feet, scampering to the door as quickly as he could, then striding down the corridor and out of the building.

Once out, he planted himself against the wall. He was panting, his vision going blurry, his head full of manic dizziness.

What was going on?

How had he just seen that man, heard that man – but Jane hadn't?

5

PARANORMAL INVESTIGATORS DEAL WITH PEOPLE WHO HAVE A range of beliefs – from adamant sceptics denying every possibility of the supernatural, to militant believers who wish to force their precarious knowledge on everyone else. Either way, people were usually furiously intrigued in what April and Julian do; although there were, of course, people who flat-out couldn't be arsed to deal with 'weirdos like them.'

Then there were their clients, who came to them with a range of emotions; from hardened outer shells to distraught, inconsolable messes.

Nancy Kemple was the latter.

This was the kind of situation where April was glad Julian was in charge, not her. She didn't deal with other people getting emotional well. She knew, of course, this was because of her own inability to deal with the emotional gravity of her past; running away from a neglectful home at fourteen, then being found by Julian at fifteen, at which point she was taught to move on from her past and harness her gifts.

Or, when she was taught to be a 'Sensitive' – as Julian called it.

But that treatment from her parents was something she had never quite dealt with, and seeing a hysterical mother weeping in front of her was a situation with which she couldn't empathise. Her cold, callous mother never shed tears over her, nor gave sympathy when April was upset, nor even noticed when April would sneak out for a few hours. Sometimes April wondered if her mother, five years later, had even noticed that she was gone.

"At first, I believed her," Nancy sobbed, taking a tissue from Julian and using it to dab her eyes. "I mean, why else would my daughter accuse her father of raping her? It's just not something she would have heard of. How could she make something like that up?"

"Of course," Julian confirmed, nodding. April enjoyed watching Julian at work, observing his caring demeanour. He was sat on the edge of the chair, looking intently at Nancy. It really showed he cared.

This, compared to April's slouched posture as she sunk into an armchair across their living room, made her feel less professional.

But it wasn't a lack of respect. April was vulnerable to the paranormal; she could sense it, sometimes even control it – and she would need both physical and emotional distance from the subject to be completely synchronised with anything that may be present.

"And then, of course, when Henry was arrested, I hated him," she continued, wiping her eyes, visibly trying to keep her composure. "And Kaylee was taken into care. But now…"

"Now what, Nancy?" Julian prompted her, speaking calmly and serenely.

"Well, then I saw my daughter. And now I know Henry is innocent."

"How do you know this?"

Nancy's face scrunched into a distorted mess. She covered her face, doing all she could to keep herself together.

"It's okay, in your own time," Julian reassured her.

Her lips pursed tightly together, her resolve strengthening, and she turned her attention entirely to Julian.

"I have looked into the eyes of my daughter every day for the past nine years," she spoke, a mixture of distress and assertion. "That *thing* – is not my daughter."

April tuned out of the conversation, listening for anything not of this world that may be whispering to her. Concentrating. Feeling the room, the house.

There was something odd about the house. It felt like it didn't belong to this family. Like they were just residents.

She closed her eyes, feeling herself sinking into her seat, the soft touch of the cushions enveloping her into a feeble embrace. The arms smelt damp, like old furniture, with a mixture of cat hair. She could taste coffee, an aroma wafting in from the kitchen.

As she opened her eyes she retained her sound mind, focusing on each one of her senses, fixing her eyes on Nancy.

There was nothing behind her, no definite vision or demon she could see. Yet, she could feel something. Something lingering in the air, something remaining from before.

Nancy's cheek transformed and contorted. Something was making an impression.

A hand-print.

The size of a child's hand, but with something thin and coarse exuding from the end of the fingers. Claws.

Closing her eyes and shaking her head, she brought herself out of her trance and refocussed her energy to the room.

"Thank you for talking to us, Nancy." Julian stood and shook her hand that loosely gripped his. "We will talk to Kaylee and see what we can find."

Julian led April outside. They walked down the porch,

along the garden path and out of the gate before they began talking.

"Anything?" Julian asked.

"Yeah," April replied. "There was a paw print on the side of her face. Like it had been made by a child, but with something coming out of the end of it. Long, sharp nails."

"So you're thinking the child is in danger?"

"That's my instinct."

Julian paused beside his car, taking a big intake of breath. April noticed him do this a lot – it was his way of making sense of things. Taking a deep breath and breathing his anxiety out. Despite believing in what he did, the job was stressful, not to mention exceedingly dangerous – you could lose more than your life; you could lose your mind or even your soul. This big intake of breath was Julian's way of uncluttering his mind.

"We need to collect the other Sensitive," Julian decided. "We need him."

"What, today?" April reacted, surprised.

"I have a feeling he'll be a help with this case. He feels like a glimpser."

"Okay, well, where do we find him?"

Julian peered around the estate, watching a group of lads cycle past, going way too fast on their bikes.

Everyone was so unaware of what the true dangers are in this world.

"We'll follow our instincts," Julian declared, getting into the car. April loyally followed.

6

THE PHARMACY QUEUE WAS ALWAYS THE LONGEST QUEUE IN THE world.

Being third in line, Oscar thought he wouldn't have to wait that long.

No.

Because at the front of the queue was an old man who had forgotten his reading glasses and was partially deaf. The pharmacist fulfilling his prescription was talking like he was speaking to a foreigner without a translator, and getting a response that was as clear as if he was talking to a cat.

Oscar still had his lingering eight-hour-shift smell clinging to him. His unfashionable green work shirt stank of dried bread and burnt bacon. It was bizarre how this smell attached itself to him, despite just working at the checkout. He would have thought he'd smell like... well, whatever checkouts smell like. But no. His aroma was that of the café beside the checkout and its wandering smells.

"You take them one a day," the pharmacist spoke slowly and clearly. "One a day. No, no, you take them one a day. Yes, you can take them today, but only take one."

Bloody hell, this is ridiculous.

All he wanted was to get his anxiety medication – and the more and more irritation this clueless old man was giving him, the more he needed it. It was like the old man was the barrier to the anxiety medication he needed because of the old man.

"Do you want a bag? A bag? I said a bag. Do you want – do you want a bag?"

Aaarrrgggghhhh.

Oscar sighed and rolled his eyes.

"Hi," came a friendly voice from beside him.

Oscar's head turned like he'd heard a gunshot.

There stood a beautiful, funky woman. Young, purple hair, a nose stud, tattoos, and a punky dress sense consisting of baggy jeans, Converse trainers and a red, sleeveless top. Her tattoos were very niche – of Tim Burton characters, and logos of various rock bands. She was immensely attractive, made even more so by her sexy, grunger image.

Oscar looked back and forth, then over his shoulder, not sure who exactly this woman was talking to.

"Erm, I'm talking to you. Hi?"

He turned back toward her. She leant casually against a shelf stocking various laxatives.

"Hi?" Oscar offered, shifting uncomfortably at the uninvited greeting from this stranger, wondering why a woman this attractive was talking to him.

"My name's April." She introduced herself with a sneaky smile that made her seem a little bit naughty. She grabbed hold of his wrist and turned his prescription so she could read his name. "And you are... Oscar Ecstavio."

She glanced to Oscar, then back to the prescription, then to Oscar. She let his wrist go, sticking out her bottom lip.

"Wow," she stated. "You so do not look like an Oscar Ecstavio. More like, I don't know – a Barney. Or a Glomp."

"I don't think Glomp's a name..." Oscar muttered, barely audible, his introverted nature taking over his quivering voice.

"Right, well, Oscar. I'm going to need you to come with me."

"Sorry?"

"I'm going to need you to come with me. You don't need all this medication and all that. There's nothing wrong with you."

Oscar's head fluttered with a thousand confused thoughts. Who was this girl? Why was she talking to him? Why did she think she knew so much about him?

"How do you know?"

"Because you're a Sensitive," she announced with a knowing grin. "It means that you can see or do things that other people can't see or do."

"Like superpowers?"

"Don't be a geek, Oscar."

The two people before him in the queue dispersed, meaning Oscar was next. He looked from the expectant pharmacist to April's raised eyebrows.

"Sorry, but I have to..." he trailed off, and shuffled forward to the counter. He could feel April behind him, watching him, not moving. He handed his prescription over and collected a bag of medication, then turned to leave. He glanced at her, giving an uncomfortable smile as he made his way to the door.

She scoffed, chuckling at his pathetic demeanour. And he felt pathetic. As he scuttled away, hunched over, walking with small steps so no one would notice him, he could feel her laughing.

He stepped into the car park and hobbled away as quickly as he could without actually running.

"It's not going to go away, you know," he heard her say, trailing a few paces behind him. "Just because you deny it, you're still going to keep seeing these things."

He glanced over his shoulder and saw her casually striding

after him. He was already out of breath, but she was just strolling a yard or two behind, keeping pace with ease.

"Leave me alone," he grunted.

"Tell me, have you been seeing things? Things you thought were there, but appeared to not be?"

The douchebag getting shot in the supermarket.

The skinhead man behind the counsellor.

"I take that silence as a yes," she decided, reaching his side.

"I need medication; I have things wrong with me."

She halted and put a hand against his chest, forcing him to come to a complete stop. He kept his head down, facing the floor, avoiding eye contact.

"I was once like you. Ridiculous, thinking there was something wrong with me. But there isn't. There's not a single thing wrong."

"Leave me alone."

"Oscar, you need to listen to me, because we need your help just as much as you need ours–"

"Please, can you just leave me alone?"

Oscar's anxiety took over. His whole body violently shook, his neck twitching. Blots appeared in his blurry vision, his head a haze of uncomfortable thoughts.

He fumbled through the bag, pulled out a packet of pills, popped a few, and shoved them into his mouth.

Still, he did not stop shaking. His eyes transfixed on the cement before him, focussing on the remains of indented gum against the pavement, the stains of human waste.

Finally seeing that he was too distressed to be in sound mind, April nodded. She withdrew a card and handed it to him, forcing it into his hand.

"Look, tell you what," she began. "If you feel like you want to actually find out who you really are, give us a call. If you want to carry on being a waste of space, then…"

She shrugged.

With a condescending pat on the back, she took off in the opposite direction.

Oscar fumbled the piece of card over. As his vision regained focus, he held it up in front him.

APRIL CRISTINE
Paranormal Investigator
07644 970306

PARANORMAL INVESTIGATOR?

He shoved the card into his back pocket and kept his head down as he shambled all the way home.

7

OSCAR TRULY COULD NOT BE ARSED WITH THE BARRAGE OF regretful diatribe his mother routinely put him through as he entered the house.

"You're living off our money!"

"You're an adult now, you know."

"You were such a smart child, what happened?"

Aren't parents supposed to encourage you? Make you feel good about yourself? Spark your dreams? It seemed this woman was intent on pulling down every bit of self-esteem he had left, trying to make it clear he would never achieve anything.

Not that he particularly had dreams. Maybe that was the problem. All that potential, such little motivation or ambition to do anything with it.

"Hi, Mum," Oscar grunted, as he did every other day. He continued the daily home-from-work routine, pulling his feet out of his shoes, dumping his bag on the floor, and tuning his mother out until she was white noise.

His father sat in the same place he was sat every day. Across the hallway and in the living room, watching either a rugby match, repetitive soaps that he only watched to perv over the attractive young women, or – if it was late enough – Babestation.

"Why won't you ever just talk to me!" his mum cried out as Oscar stomped upstairs.

Because why would I want to talk to someone who tells me I'm a failure every day?

Slamming the door of his bedroom and feeling like he was fourteen again, he dove onto the bed and pulled the pillow over his head.

It had been a long day. Just as long as every other day.

Soon, he would enter his nightly routine. Masturbate, watch television, play on the Xbox until 3.00 a.m., then lie awake in bed until he had to get up for work.

But something distracted his mind.

That girl. April.

She had told Oscar there was nothing wrong with him.

She was the first person to ever say that.

But she didn't know him. Maybe if she did get to know him, realise what he was truly like, her perception of him would change. Within a few days she would solemnly declare, "Sorry, Oscar, I was wrong – you are a fuck-up, you do need that medication, you are a dick."

It's true. Anyone who thought he wasn't a self-indulgent nobody just evidently hadn't gotten to know him that well.

She was incredibly pretty though. Had that really kooky, punky thing going on. It was sexy.

Checking his door was locked, he slipped down his trousers, laid on his bed and daydreamed about April.

He thought about kissing her. About running his hands down her purple hair, brushing down her unblemished immaculate tattooed skin. Thought about the curves of her body, the way her kooky fashion sense only made her sexier.

"Oscar."

Oscar's head turned quicker than a bullet. He abruptly lifted his trousers from around his ankles, holding his belt around his waist, fully alert.

But there was no one there.

Just his bedroom, clothes on the floor, and his poster of Megan Fox on the wall.

Taking another moment to survey the room with a scrutinising inspection of every corner, he concluded it was in his head. There was nothing there.

He laid down.

Relaxed once more.

Pictured April. That smile. It had made him melt. It was perfectly curved, making her look cute yet naughty.

Those lips.

Those luscious lips.

Those piercings.

"*Oscar!*"

He shot to his feet, his eyes wide open, his vision darting to every crevasse and every shadow.

Now I know I heard that!

The voice had screamed his name with a venomously low pitch.

But the voice had gone. The room was empty.

He refastened his belt and searched his room, constantly looking around, lifting up every stray item of clothing and every open video game case.

His room was a confined mess, with little places anyone could hide. After checking in his wardrobe and under the bed, he concluded he was alone.

But he wasn't.

He couldn't be.

Someone had screamed his name. Far too deep to be his mother's voice, and with far too much vigour for the little energy his dad could muster.

"Get a grip!" he barked at himself.

He knew he was being pathetic. This was why he took medication. His anxiety manifested itself in many ways. Given, he had never 'heard voices' before – but he had seen things in the corner of his eye that disappeared when he looked at them, felt a brush of wind in a sealed room. How was this any different?

Maybe he'd think about April later.

He sat at his desk and opened his laptop lid.

A scream roared out from the speakers so loud it sent him flying off the chair. A dark face stared back at him in place of his email, with gaping holes encompassing hollow shadows and bloody scars ripping its flesh.

Oscar fumbled back to his feet.

It was gone.

With a vigorous pace he shut down the web page, shut down the laptop, and switched off the plug.

It took him a few minutes until he realised he was still stood in the middle of his room, the four small walls closing in on him, his breathing accelerating with forceful unease.

What the fuck is going on?

That guy in the supermarket.

The counsellor's boyfriend.

The disgusting, scarred face taking over the Internet.

Then April. The person who said she had an explanation. The one who said she could tell him what was happening.

The one who said he was worth more than this.

Fumbling his hand through his pocket, he withdrew the card and looked upon it once more.

A paranormal investigator.

This was crazy.

I need drugs, not 'Ghostbusters.'

Closing his eyes with a perturbed sigh, he bowed his head and contemplated.

Weird shit kept happening.

How else could he explain it?

Because I'm crazy.

Still.

This made sense, in a disturbing kind of way.

Fuck it.

He grabbed his mobile phone and dialled the number.

8

To say April was apprehensive was an understatement.

Was this kid really the all-powerful Sensitive Julian had sensed?

Had she gotten the right guy?

Because he seemed like a dipshit loser.

He had scruffy clothes too big for him hanging off his scrawny body, ruffled hair that looked like it had never been touched by gel or shampoo, and a nervous disposition, which meant he was too easily intimidated to even look her in the eye.

Then, not to mention, the ridiculous phone call she had received from him.

"Er, this is Oscar, the guy at the pharmacy. Er, I don't know why I'm calling. Er, this is April, right?"

If he had said er one more time, April was pretty sure she would have thrown the phone across the room.

Now there he was, stumbling out of his parents' house, his hands in his pockets and his head down. There was no one around to intimidate him, yet he still couldn't lift his head up to face the world. It seemed like she and Julian had more to mould than just his Sensitive powers – they had to stop him from being such an infuriating mess.

Seriously, how was she supposed to work with this guy?

Even the way he opened the car door and sat down on the seat reeked of social awkwardness. He slouched, sticking his hands into his pockets, staring at the gear stick. It was as if he wanted to look at her, but couldn't lift his head high enough, so he just focussed on something lower down beside her instead.

April raised her eyebrows and smiled, waiting for him to say the first words.

"I…" he began. "I don't know why I'm here."

"Well that's a start," April said, more patronisingly than she'd intended.

"I – I keep seeing things."

"Yes, you do," April confirmed. "That's because you're what we call a Sensitive."

"What's a Sensitive?"

April exhaled with sheer exasperation. Was she this much work for Julian when he'd found her and trained her?

She was a damaged teenager living on the streets, but still – at least she wasn't so irritating.

"A Sensitive is called a Sensitive because they are Sensitive to the paranormal and the supernatural. You are Sensitive to the world of the unliving."

"You mean, dead people?"

"Not exclusively but yes, sometimes. Sometimes demons."

Oscar snorted with amusement.

April did all she could to contain her irritation at his reaction. It would be the same for any sceptic who heard this news for the first time.

"Have you ever seen anything strange, Oscar? Something you can't explain? Maybe you've seen or heard something no one else has?"

"… Yes."

"This isn't because you have anxiety. You don't need this ridiculous medication you're taking. You need to be taught to hone these skills."

Oscar sighed. April could see the thoughts twisting and turning inside him, so clearly torn between whether to take a leap of faith or to rely on his ingrained rational thinking.

"Is it just you?"

"Me and Julian. He's a sound guy; just don't piss him off and you'll be fine."

"And what powers do you have?" He spoke so softly, it was as if he didn't want to believe he was asking it.

"My Sensitive is that I can sense and feel the paranormal. I can also act as a conduit."

"A what?"

"A conduit. It means I let spooky fuckers borrow my body."

"What about Julian?"

"He can see Sensitive powers in others. And he's a kick-arse exorcist."

Oscar raised his eyebrows. She could see he was over-whelmed, entwined with disbelief.

"Yo, Oscar, can you lift your head up and look at me, yeah?" April decided she needed to take a different tact. If only to stop him pissing her off, this was something he was going to need to see to believe.

Oscar lifted his head slowly, but still didn't meet April's eyes.

"A little bit more," she prompted. "Almost there. Look me in the eyes, not the chest."

She grinned as he blushed. He slowly lifted his head, warily making brief eye contact with her, shifting his glance back and forth.

"I'm going to take you to a case we're working on," she

decided. "Maybe when you meet this little girl, you'll be able to see something others can't. Maybe then you'll believe."

"… Okay," he muttered.

Rolling her eyes at his despondency, she put the car into gear.

Does this guy get enthusiastic about anything? He's about to see a sodding demon, for Christ's sake! She sped off, smirking as Oscar gripped his seat and quickly fastened his seatbelt.

9

To say Oscar felt awkward was an understatement. The whole drive, April kept shooting glances at him as if she was studying him or trying to figure him out. It was difficult enough that he found her immensely attractive, but trying not to stare at her staring was proving difficult.

After a drive that felt longer than it was, April pulled up outside an old-fashioned building. The summer evening had turned to night, and there was an uncomfortable humidity lingering in the air. The building itself was grand, with spiralling architecture and red bricks covered in green moss.

"What is this place?" Oscar enquired.

"This is the place where social services dump kids they don't know what to do with," April answered in a glumly matter-of-fact tone.

"Why are we here?"

"Because this is where they are keeping the girl we're going to meet."

April hastily stepped out of the car, stylishly using the roof to lever herself out. Oscar did the same, though without the slick manoeuvre. Instead, he stumbled over the door and just about kept his balance.

A man who looked a few years older than April approached, his eyes in a fixed glare at Oscar. Oscar even glanced over his shoulder to check this guy was looking at him. There was no one else there.

"This is Julian," April introduced. "He's the boss."

He was a good-looking guy, no doubt about it. His hair was swept back to his neck; he had a prim, clean-shaven face and a well-toned physique that made Oscar feel instantly inferior. Still, he didn't want to get on the wrong side of this guy, so he offered a hand.

"Nice to meet you. I'm Oscar."

Julian looked at Oscar's hand like he was being offered shit on a cake, prompting Oscar to immediately withdraw it. Julian didn't smile; in fact, quite the opposite. He looked at everything like it was a mediocre speck of dirt he simply needed to tread over.

"Follow us," Julian demanded, his voice assertive, but with a rugged huskiness. "And don't say a word unless instructed to."

Julian turned and strode to the decadently majestic front door, pushing its heavy weight open with relative ease. Even the way he walked was at a superior pace. A natural leader, someone who automatically willed the weak to follow him – the complete opposite of Oscar.

"He takes some warming to," April commented as she followed Julian, and Oscar fumbled after them.

"We are here to see Kaylee Kemple," Julian informed the lady at the desk. This lady glanced at Julian, then averted her wary gaze to April's niche dress sense, then to Oscar's shy exterior.

"That girl is being kept under strict protection," the woman answered.

"I know she is, her lawyers sent us," Julian interrupted

confidently. "We have an appointment to see her. If there's an issue, perhaps you could take it up with her police liaison officer."

Any gumption the lady thought she had faded, and she nodded warily.

"Okay," she confirmed. "But I do warn you, that girl – she isn't right."

"Can you point us the way please?"

"Okay." The woman nodded feverishly, her eyes wide open, as if she was shocked that people were willingly speaking to this girl. "Down the corridor, fourth door on the right."

Julian gave her a slight nod, then strode forward again, leading the way.

Oscar scuffled to April's side.

"Who is this girl?" he asked.

"This girl claims her dad raped her," April answered mono-syllabically. "Her mum and dad are claiming she didn't. They want us to see if there is anything 'off' about her."

"Off?"

"As in, anything untoward." They paused outside the door. "Not of this world. Demonic. Keep your eyes open, Oscar – if you can see things, and this girl is surrounded by these particular forces, then you will likely see things in this room that you can't explain. Be wary – if it's the first time you see them, you might be in for a shock."

Oscar's jaw remained open as he nodded with absent eyes and a terror-filled mind. What was it he was going to see?

I don't want to see things!

He wished he was back at home. In his bed. Something he never thought he'd wish in a million years.

Julian knocked on the door a few times, laid his hand carefully on the door handle, and twisted it. The door creaked open, and Julian stepped toward a dark figure in the corner.

April gestured Oscar in and shut the door behind them. She led him to a chair behind Julian and sat next to him.

The room was marginally lit by the moon seeping through a narrow gap in the curtain. Besides that, there were many shadows and many pitch-black corners Oscar grew increasingly wary of. There was an eclipsed figure across the room, sat on a bed made up of a single mattress and a wired, metallic frame. This figure was encased in black and barely moved. The silhouette was in the shape of a young girl, but the way it breathed, moved ever-so-slightly, sinisterly twisting its head – it did not feel like a young girl.

"Julian will try and talk to it," April whispered to Oscar. "We need to sit back and watch, then report on what we see."

"Hello," Julian greeted the dark figure.

A croaky, deep-pitched chuckle responded.

"How old is she?" Oscar whispered to April.

"Nine," April responded.

"Then how is her voice so deep?"

April didn't answer. Oscar was pleased she didn't. As soon as the question escaped his lips, he knew he didn't want it answered.

"Can I ask who I am talking to?" Julian prompted, standing tall a few steps away from the bed the little girl propped itself upon.

"Kaylee," the girl responded in a high-pitched, girly voice – but a little too girly, as if it was someone imitating how a girl's voice should sound. It made Oscar's entire body shudder.

"No," Julian stated, shaking his head. "No, I want your real name."

"Kaylee," it responded again, with the exact same tone of voice. "My name is Kaylee."

As Oscar's eyes adjusted to the light, he could just about make out some of the girl's face. Except, the facial features didn't seem like that of a girl. Yes, they were a girl's nose, a girl's mouth, and a girl's eyes – but something about them was off. As if her features were being manipulated into a knowing snarl.

Cuts marked her face, open slits that were yet to close hanging open upon her.

"My daddy molested me," the girl sang, in a happy-go-lucky sing-song voice. It was strange, how such a dramatic, awful accusation was blurted out with such a playful happiness.

"Molested?" Julian responded, sticking his bottom lip out. "That's a big word. Where have you heard that word before, Kaylee?"

"My daddy does it all the time," she sang out again with a buoyant grin. "He molests me all the time."

Something else was there. Oscar was starting to make it out. Something in the shadows around the girl. Something with hazy, indefinite lines, towering over her, consuming the air that surrounded her fuzzy hair.

"What is it?" April whispered. "Are you seeing something?"

"Are you seeing it too?" Oscar asked, growing scared.

"I can feel it, I can smell it – but I can't see it," April confirmed. "Can you see it?"

Oscar stared at a slight movement in the shadows. A cloud of grey breath became momentarily visible, and it petrified him. His hands gripped the side of his chair, his entire body stiffening.

"Yes." Oscar nodded profusely. "Yes, I can."

"Is Kaylee in there with you?" Julian continued. "Is she in there, right now?"

"I am Kaylee."

"No, you're not. You look like Kaylee. You sound like Kaylee. You may even sometimes act like Kaylee. But you are not Kaylee, are you?"

Silence.

The creature behind her moved once more.

It grew larger. A looming shadow, creeping up the walls, creeping over the ceiling, growing larger, coming toward Oscar, coming toward him faster and faster.

His paralysed body shook, seizing in terror.

That's when he saw it.

A female figure, long, black hair reaching down to its waist, large breasts that consumed half its chest, thick black lips – except its eyes were less female. They curved inward to large, dilated pupils that grew to the entire vicinity of its eyes. Below its navel, its waist turned into a long tail, like that of a snake. This tail slithered out, consuming the room, at least three times the size of its torso.

Then in its arms. A baby. Squeezing tightly onto it. The tail wrapping itself around the baby's neck, lifting the baby up, holding it in mid-air.

Oscar could feel April's eyes on him as his eyes grew wider and wider, and his fingers dug further into the arm of the chair.

He didn't notice her stares, nor the fact that Julian and the little girl had now turned their attention to his screams. He couldn't even feel the screams exuding from his throat. He couldn't feel the soreness they were creating, couldn't hear the echoing of his wails around the room.

"Oscar, calm down," April insisted, but the words just blurred into the background with the rest of the room.

The creature loomed further and further over Oscar.

Then the baby it asphyxiated with its tail moved. Its head rotated toward him, its eyes just like its owner – black, full. Its face a ravenous growl. Its mouth open.

It was an abyss of black matter, thinly pointed fangs curling out, dripping with excess saliva.

Oscar fell to the ground, stumbled to his feet, and ran for his life.

1 0

Oscar burst out the door and fell to his knees. Before he could even register his need to gag, he was throwing up over a well-laid flower bed, retching repeatedly.

The acidic gunk of his vomit lurched up his throat once more, forcing him to blurt out another mouthful.

He clambered to his knees and attempted to balance himself. The whole world was spinning around him. The house, the lawn, the gravel, spinning and spinning, until he felt so dizzy he was sick again.

"Yo, Oscar!"

Oscar lifted his head with a jolt, expecting to see the beast once more. But it wasn't the beast – it was April. Crouching down beside him, putting a hand on his back.

He hadn't heard her approach, but somehow she was at his side.

At that moment, he wished he could be anywhere else. He felt his cheeks burn red. He bowed his head in humiliation that April had to see him puking over a family's garden.

"Oh, Jesus," she declared, frowning at the destroyed flower

bed. "You could have at least aimed it away from the roses. They probably took friggin' ages to do, too."

Oscar slumped onto his arse, grimacing at the pain of the bumps of the drive-way digging into him. He shook his head, willing himself to overcome his embarrassment and ask the questions he wanted answered.

"What was that?" Oscar gasped between hyperventilating pants.

"Just breathe, dude," April reassured him, patting his back. "Just keep breathing."

The door creaked open and Julian took a few judgemental steps toward Oscar.

"How bad is it?" Julian prompted.

"Oh, about five times worse than my first demon," April decided. "About ten times worse than your average pussy. I mean, seriously, dude, the orchids?"

Oscar pushed April's hand off him, not taking kindly to the ill-timed jokes. He felt enough of a tit already. He went to stand in a spurt of anger but only ended up stumbling onto his back.

"What was that?" he demanded once more.

"All will be explained," Julian announced, pressing a button on his car keys to unlock his car. "We need to get you home first. Get you a glass of water."

"You want to take me *home*? After I've seen *that*?"

"Not your home, doofus," April sighed. "Back to our home."

"I don't even know you people."

"Yes, you don't," Julian agreed. "But as it is, we are the only ones who will believe you saw what you just saw. Everyone else will call you a delusional prick. We, however, need to know what you saw to identify what demon we are dealing with – so, to us, you are a helpful prick. So, what's it going to be?"

Julian turned to Oscar and gave an award-winning smile, his white teeth sparkling.

"Are you going to be a delusional prick or a helpful prick?"

Oscar's breathing slowed down. It was nowhere near calm, but he could at least take in his surroundings without becoming nauseous. He glanced from April to Julian, and back to April.

"Fine," he grunted. "Just – take me anywhere but here."

April offered Oscar a hand and helped him up.

"See, bud?" she grinned at him. "You're not as much of an irritating cowardly dick as I thought."

Oscar frowned, not sure whether to take that as a compliment. She helped him hobble to the back seat of the car, which he climbed into and laid down upon.

For the whole drive, Oscar stared at the roof of the car. All he could see were the ghastly eyes of whatever it was that he saw. If following these people meant he was going to see more of that, he wasn't entirely sure it was for him.

11

EVERYTHING HENRY HAD HEARD ABOUT PRISON WAS TRUE.

Even though he was only in holding, being denied bail – it was still full of people that terrified him with a glance. He was a middle-class family man. A doctor. He had never mixed with drug dealers or criminals before, and it was wearing him down.

The constant looking over his shoulder. The knowing there was nothing he could do if he saw something over his shoulder. The unbearable tension of how he might be woken up the next morning.

But the most unbearable thought was knowing that he was innocent, yet still stuck there.

And that there was nothing he could do about it.

Once again, he was restrained and guided out of his cell, down the vacant corridors, to another interrogation room. Another desk, with another tape recorder, with another interview, with a blank police officer trying not to be judgemental despite having automatically presumed him guilty.

This police officer allowed silence to fill the room before he started. He was methodical in his approach – making sure his pad was out, his pen was ready, and the tape rewound to the beginning.

Finally, giving a vacant look to Henry, the police officer began the tape.

"This is Detective Inspector Jason Lyle, interviewing Doctor Henry Kemple. The time is twenty fifty-eight. It is noted that Doctor Kemple has waived his right to have his attorney present. We'll begin."

Henry let out a deep breath he didn't realise he was holding. He tried to relax his tense muscles, only to find that they tensed again a moment later.

"Doctor Kemple–"

"Call me Henry, please," Henry interrupted. "You're not a patient, Henry will do."

"Henry," Jason corrected himself. "Could you just explain briefly why you have waived your right to an attorney, just out of interest?"

"Because I am innocent," Henry pleaded. He thought he was sounding assertive, but in truth, he came across as desperate. His voice was soft-spoken, like a caring father; nothing like the hardened criminal he was being made to feel. "I'm tired of these ridiculous impromptu interrogations. Why am I here?"

"Because I am taking over this case, Henry," Jason answered, noting something down on his pad. "And I just wanted to find out a bit more about you."

"A bit more about me?" Henry repeated, shaking his head, wiping his tears on his sleeve because he couldn't lift his restrained hands to his eyes. "I'm a doctor, a husband – and a father! I love my family. What do you need to know?"

"Your daughter is saying you molested her, Henry. She is nine years old. Why would she accuse you of such a thing?"

"I don't know."

"Could she have heard the word 'molest' in the playground, perhaps?"

"I don't know."

"I just seems a strange thing to accuse–"

"I don't *know*!"

Jason rested the end of his pen in his mouth, his eyes hovering over Henry as if inspecting a difficult clue. Henry did not know what to make of this officer. He was unlike the rest, though Henry couldn't decide how.

"I understand your attorneys have called in a group of paranormal investigators," Jason offered, again keeping his expression null and his voice flat.

"Have they?"

"What do you think they are hoping to find?"

"How would I know?"

"Have you seen your daughter since your arrest?"

Henry's weary face morphed into a passionate frown. Scowling at Jason through gritted teeth, he felt his nails dig into his hands in frustration.

"How the hell would I see her?" Henry's lip quivered, his eyes welling up, his emotions spilling from his feeble mind to his fatigued face. "When you are accusing me of doing such things as – as you are accusing."

"Because I went to see her the other day, Henry."

"Oh yeah?"

"What kind of girl is your daughter?"

Henry vehemently shook his head.

"What's that got to do with anything?" he protested.

"Please, Henry, just answer the question."

Henry closed his eyes, clearing his mind, doing all he could to contain his inconsolable grief at this ridiculous situation.

"She is a happy girl, a delightful girl. Friendly, outgoing, boisterous. The life and soul of the party. Would never say a nasty thing about anyone."

Jason nodded as if this was confirming something, though Henry couldn't figure out what.

"When I met your daughter–" he began, then paused. Taking a moment of clear thought, he stopped the recording.

"What are you doing?" Henry asked, shocked at this lack of procedure.

"When I met your daughter, Henry," Jason continued, ignoring Henry's brief outrage, "she was anything but happy. She was far from boisterous. And she was definitely not the life and soul of the party."

"What are you saying?" Henry pleaded.

"I'm saying, whatever your investigating friends find… It's not that I believe in that kind of thing, it's just… I…"

"Officer, if there is something you are trying to say?"

Jason looked around the room. He straightened his sleeves, smoothed down his collar, and clasped his hands over his mouth. Then, after finally gathering his thoughts, he turned his gaze to Henry.

"Whatever is in that room, it's not… What I'm trying to say, Henry, is that I believe you. I think you're innocent."

1 2

JULIAN SLAMMED A NOTEBOOK AND PEN ON THE TABLE BEFORE Oscar and stood, arms folded, gazing at him inquisitively.

"What do you want from me?" Oscar pleaded.

"You saw the demon," Julian replied, a dead stare and a flat voice. "Now we need to know what we are dealing with."

"I didn't see a demon!" Oscar claimed. "I just saw something because I have mental issues. I'm batshit crazy, I'm off my rocker, I'm–"

"Oscar," April interrupted, leaning coolly against the far wall, her voice coated with relaxation. So much confidence, so much control; Oscar envied it.

He realised he was sweating. Panting, even. Looking back and forth at these two people. Julian, standing expectantly with a bored look on his face; it wasn't even impatience, it was an expectant wait for Oscar to get his shit together. April was a little different. She had a tinge of a smirk, as if she found the whole thing amusing.

Neither of them were anywhere near as out of sorts as Oscar was.

Finally, he forced his heavy breathing to subside and willed himself to raise himself to their level.

"The demon," Julian demanded. "What did it look like?"

"Erm, okay…" Oscar began, resolved to comply. "It was a woman."

Oscar looked back at Julian expectantly, who returned his stare with a close of the eyes that accompanied a sigh and a raise of the eyebrows.

"There are many, many female demons, Oscar," Julian pointed out, speaking as if he were addressing a petulant child. "We are going to need you to be a little more specific than that."

"Erm, okay, okay." Oscar's thoughts shot through his mind as he frantically tried to make sense of them. He willed himself to somehow focus on the inexplicable image of what he had seen. "Long hair. She – she wasn't wearing her top. I mean, she had breasts out and everything."

Julian raised an eyebrow to April, who sniggered knowingly.

"She had no legs. It was like her bottom half was turning into a tail, like a snake's tail, like she was half-snake, half-woman."

Julian clicked his fingers and instantly picked out an old, broken, leather-bound, dusty book off a shelf behind him and started sifting through the pages.

"Go on," he prompted.

"Okay, I – I don't know what else to say."

"Was she holding anything?"

Oscar paused for thought, thinking carefully.

"Actually, yes," he answered. "She was holding – I think it was a baby."

Julian nodded, opened the book, and slammed it in front of Oscar. It was open to a page that displayed a woman exactly like the one he had described.

"Oh my God," he choked. "That's her!"

April moseyed over and peered at the page. She got very close to Oscar. He could faintly smell her and it made him nervous.

"We got a name?" April prompted, forcing Oscar to return his focus to the demon.

"Yes," Julian replied, smiling as if demonology was his time to shine. "She has had various names, known as Ardat Lili, or Lilitu – or, most commonly, Lilith."

"Lilith?" Oscar echoed. April shushed him.

"She is a succubus, associated mainly with either pregnant women or young children, hence the child."

Oscar feebly raised his hands, and the other two looked at him as if he were an idiot.

"Sorry, but – what's a succubus?" he innocently asked.

"A female demon that shags blokes, often when they are asleep," April answered matter-of-factly.

Oscar nodded, not sure what to make of that information.

"Around 4000 BC," Julian continued, "she was reported as a water-demon. More recently, however, from a stone carving in 2400 BC, it was claimed that she was having sex with various men to unleash her demon-spawn upon the world."

Oscar looked from April to Julian, to April, and back to Julian again.

Was he in some kind of fantasy world?

They were aware this was reality, right?

He shook his head. His thoughts filled with utter confusion.

What the fuck are these people on...

"She has a Sumerian origin," Julian began to conclude, Oscar nodding as if he knew what that meant. "She's a sexual demon, often preying on the young, killing children, drinking blood, and raping men. Most notably, she is part of a pairing, with a similar male demon."

"There's more of them?" Oscar choked, bemused, only to find his irritating comment ignored.

"Lilith is often referred to as a female, but she has a male counterpart – usually referred to as Lilu."

"So where does that leave us?" April asked, taking a seat next to Oscar, not noticing how distracted Oscar was by her smooth skin, her well-fitted strappy top, and her generous cleavage.

Noticing Julian's frown, Oscar quickly diverted his attention away from her.

"Well, knowing the kind of horrific things this demon does to young children, and to men – I'd say we need to act fast. God knows what this thing will have done already."

FINALLY, JASON COULD REST FOR A MOMENT. HE'D BEEN RUSHED off his feet for most of the day, solving this and that, answering question after question.

It was part of his job, and it was not a problem – but it was nice to finally be able to get himself a coffee.

The kitchen of the police station was smaller than most cells, with a noisy kettle, an aged microwave, and a toaster where you have to hold the button down to make it work. Unfortunately, updating and repairing kitchen equipment was not the priority of a detective inspector, nor was it within the police budget.

As he left the kitchen, sipping his coffee and thinking how much he detests the supermarket brand stuff, one of his sergeants came bustling up to him.

"Hey," called the man, getting Jason's attention. "Can you sign this?"

Giving his colleague his coffee to hold, Jason traded it for a few pages attached to a clipboard. As he glanced down at it, he suddenly became alert.

"What is this?" Jason demanded.

"What do you mean?"

"This is talking about Henry Kemple's release."

"Didn't you hear? His daughter dropped the charges, he's being released."

What?

What could have prompted such a sudden change in the daughter's story?

And how could this information have gone past him?

"No," Jason spat. "I did *not* hear."

Shoving the clipboard against his inferior, Jason marched through the corridors and to the front desk of the station.

"The Kemples?" he barked at the clueless officer sitting at the desk.

"Sorry?"

"The Kemples, being released. Where are they?"

"Er, I think the mum's through there–" he pointed a loose finger down a corridor. Jason had begun marching down the corridor before the officer could say another word.

Storming forward, he looked through the window of every room. Eventually, he reached the one where he spotted Nancy's distraught face and entered.

"Mrs Kemple," Jason began, quietly shutting the door, and taking a seat opposite her. "I've just heard. What's happened?"

Nancy dabbed at her eyes with a tissue as she shrugged her shoulders.

"Kaylee claimed she was lying," she answered, shaking her head as if disbelieving it.

"Do you trust her?" Jason inquired.

Nancy took a moment to consider this question.

"I believe that Henry is innocent. That he didn't touch her. I know that much."

"So, what is the matter then?"

Nancy closed her eyes and sighed, furiously shaking her head. She went to speak a few times, each time producing nothing but dead air. Eventually, she took a deep breath in, composed herself, and answered the question.

"It's Kaylee," she spoke softly. "She's – she's not herself. She's changed. And I don't completely understand why."

"Maybe she's playing up for some reason. Kids can often be naughty."

"Have you met my daughter, Detective Inspector?"

Jason shuddered at the recollection of those few moments he had spent in Kaylee's presence.

"Yes," he confirmed, directing his eye contact elsewhere. "Yes, I have."

"And tell me – did she seem all right to you?"

Jason returned Nancy's adamant stare, considering how to respond to that question. Kaylee hadn't appeared to be your average conflicted or traumatised little girl. The room she was in had turned cold; she gave an aura of menace, and there was a deeply sinister glint in her eye. For a nine-year-old girl, there was nothing innocent or childish about her.

"I – I don't know how to answer that question," Jason answered honestly.

"Well, let me tell you about Kaylee. Kaylee is the kind of girl who would let another child have the last sweet in the sweet shop so that child doesn't get upset. Kaylee is the kind of girl who draws pictures of flowers and gives them to her teacher. Kaylee is the kind of girl who smiles and she lights up the room. Did she smile while you were there?"

"... Yes."

"And what was that smile like?"

Jason shrugged his shoulders despondently.

"It – I don't know how to put it into words."

"Exactly."

Jason tucked his shirt in and pulled his tie up, having to do something with his hands to avoid nervously fidgeting. He knew exactly what she was saying, but still needed to maintain an air of professionalism. Ridiculing a young child was not appropriate for a police officer of his standing.

"Look, Mrs Kemple, maybe things will clear themselves up in time. But you are getting your husband back, and you are getting your daughter back – this is surely a good thing. Just take your time to be happy about that."

Nancy dabbed her eyes once more and dropped her gaze to the floor.

Jason was so convincing, he almost believed his reassurance himself.

14

Nancy could see herself in the eyes of those who walked past her.

Although she could not directly see her reflection, she knew she was a mess. People's faces were etched with discomfort and avoidance, looking at her as if she was a homeless urchin just picked up off the street.

She wasn't a homeless urchin. Nor had she been picked up off the street.

She was a distressed, concerned mother – who simply did not understand what was happening.

Despite initial concerns, she hadn't doubted her husband. Even after Kaylee persisted in her accusations, she remained firm in the belief that Henry had not touched their daughter, nor had the thought ever even crossed his mind.

But she hadn't completely disbelieved Kaylee either. It was as if it was a lie that Kaylee had convinced herself so adamantly was real that, to her, it was a truth.

In a situation when someone isn't being honest with themselves, how are they meant to be honest with anyone else?

It's just... Kaylee had never heard the word 'molest' before.

She didn't even know about sex, what it was, or where she came from; she knew far too little to even approach a subject such as rape.

Nancy decided to put her faith in the group her lawyers had contacted – The Sensitives, she recalled them being referred to. As much as she reminded herself she didn't believe in such things, in a time of crisis one's thoughts jump to extreme conclusions.

A girl walked out and Nancy's body tensed. She filled with terror, desperately on edge to see her daughter's face.

Then the girl walked past, with a different face to her daughter's, into the arms of a different father.

And she relaxed.

Is this really how I'm going to be when I see my daughter again? Worried and on edge?

She bowed her head and closed her eyes. Despaired about what kind of mother she was to doubt her family so much. Never had she thought she'd dread seeing father and daughter reunited.

But there she was.

A pair of weakened eyes appeared from a far door. A man once strong, but full of the emotions of weeks in a jail cell, cautiously stepped into the corridor.

Nancy rose. Not sure why, she just automatically stood.

It felt like the right thing to do.

Her eyes met her husband's.

And they broke.

So many nights sleeping in their home alone. No daughter to cuddle, no husband to cry to. Just the sound of late-night television to help her fall asleep.

After all that, this is what she does.

Stands across the corridor of a sparsely populated police station reception, staring vehemently at the eyes of the man she vowed to love, in sickness and in health.

He froze too, casting a solemn tear from his eye, letting it dance slowly down his cheek.

"Henry–" Nancy began, stepping forward to embrace him – but the gesture was cut short by the sound of their daughter running into the room.

"Daddy!" Kaylee cried, a face full of elation. Despite running out of the doorway closest to Nancy, she bypassed her and sprinted straight into her father's arms.

Nancy could only watch as Henry fell to her level and clutched his arms tightly around Kaylee. He fell to pieces, his lip quivering and his eyes filling with tears. His arms gripped her, holding her closely, clinging on for dear life. It was an embrace that never ended, one that was flooded with the emotions of the love between father and daughter.

Nancy remained stationary, watching.

It made sense that Kaylee ran past her, and straight to her father.

Didn't it?

Can't think such destructive thoughts now. Pull yourself together.

Willing herself to be strong, to keep faith in her family, she forced a forged smile to her lips. She went to step forward but was stopped as Kaylee and Henry pulled apart.

They remained close and, in exact unison, turned their heads toward Nancy. A sadistic smile crept across both of their faces. Something shared, unbeknownst to Nancy, was passed across in the silent subconscious between father and daughter.

Or maybe Nancy was just being paranoid.

Yes.

Weeks of stress accumulating into bad thoughts. That's all it was.

Just the emotions she had kept bottled up for so long, finally reaching the surface.

Then Kaylee turned to Henry and, keeping her eyes pinned

on her mother's, whispered something gently into her father's ear.

Henry nodded.

And the moment was over.

Henry took Kaylee by the hand toward Nancy, allowing mother and daughter to finally embrace. It wasn't a tight, desperate hug like she had given her father – but rather a reluctant, compulsory hug you would give an aunt you barely see.

Nancy willed the bad thoughts to the back of her mind.

She told herself it was nothing. Just a silly interpretation of a love between Henry and Kaylee that, really, they should be celebrating.

Her father had his daughter back again.

And the mother had her family.

No more sleepless nights alone.

Or so she thought.

15

IF YOU ASKED OSCAR WHY HE ENTERTAINED THE RIDICULOUS notions of him having some special supernatural abilities, he probably couldn't give you an answer. He had no idea why he remained in the same room as Julian and April, listening to them prattle on about demons and exorcisms and ghosts.

Maybe it was because April was really attractive. Maybe that's what it was.

Maybe it was because he had found somewhere he belonged, which was something he'd never had. At school, he'd had plenty of acquaintances, but never many friends. Various social groups he may have had lunch with, but never anyone he would invite to his house for tea, or down the park for a kickabout.

Maybe it was because it finally gave him a purpose. Something these people genuinely believed he could do, no matter how preposterous a concept as him being a 'Sensitive' with special paranormal powers may be. These people actually wanted him there. He hardly had huge ambitions of climbing up the promotion ladder in the supermarket. This gave his insignificant life some significance.

But, most likely, it was because it felt right. Like somewhere deep inside of him, it was true. It was a feeling he couldn't articulate – hell, he could barely acknowledge it – but it offered him an explanation. Something that provided reasons to the various mental ailments he had been diagnosed with and medicated for.

So he watched as Julian and April fervently paced the room, distressed about the news of a phone call Julian had received.

"I can't quite believe this," Julian had announced as he returned to the room.

"What?" inquired April, moving to the edge of her chair in anticipation.

"Kaylee Kemple has changed her testimony. She's saying she lied about her dad, and they are both being released."

Oscar watched April for some direction as to how he should act. April's jaw dropped and she looked around the room for imaginary answers, which told Oscar that he should evidently be shocked also.

Though, if this girl was in fact 'possessed,' as they were hypothesizing, surely she'd be erratic in her decisions. Changing her mind and coming up with precarious accusations that would mess with the family seemed like a perfect way to torment them. And why else would a demon be plaguing this family, other than to torment them?

April and Julian were on their feet. They had a huge whiteboard against the wall, and a dozen pens scattered around various furniture surfaces, and they wasted little time in filling it. Everything they knew went on it. Starting with the basics: the girl, the parents, their ages, their jobs, their family history. Then they mindmapped off Kaylee's name, noting various observations they had made about her.

Oscar became mesmerized with April's buttocks for a short period of time, watching them bounce and wobble hypnotically with a dainty enticement as she wrote various pieces of information on the board. After a few moments, he broke himself out of his daze and forced himself to focus on what she had written.

In a big red pen, she had written in capitalised letters, *LILITH / ARDAT LILI*, and joined it to Kaylee's name. Around these two main headings, various pieces of information had been noted.

Cold room in her presence.

Repeated "Daddy molested me."

Smile unlike a child's normal smile.

After the board was full, Oscar watched statically as Julian and April vocally came to life, bouncing questions back and forth. They ignored Oscar sitting there, staring at them.

"So why would she claim he molested her in the first place?" April proposed.

"To mess with the dad," Julian answered. "But then why would she stop messing with the dad?"

"Where's the mum in all this?"

"Has she made any accusations toward her?"

"I don't know, has she?"

"Not that I know of."

"Hey, guys—" Oscar tried to interject, but his timid offering was cancelled out by the relentless wave of questions.

"What's the link here?"

"The link between what?"

"Lilith, the demon, and the accusations?"

"Is there ever really a link?"

"The demon often molested men itself…"

"Maybe it's planning something?"

"Maybe—" Oscar tried again.

"I think—"

"Hey, guys!" Oscar shouted.

April and Julian froze, slowly rotating their heads toward

him in unison, taken aback by the interjection of his impudent voice.

"Maybe she just needs to be closer to her parents to continue her attack," Oscar offered, then sat back in his chair, curling up, retracting back into his introverted shell.

Julian looked to April. It was the kind of look that said, *He's right, but I really don't want to admit it.*

"Of course," April spoke. "If this is just the first wave of attacks, surely she's going to need to be closer to her parents for the rest?"

They continued barking back and forth various ideas and plans and concoctions.

Oscar just sat back in his chair, smiling, glad to actually be of some use.

16

Everyone has their way to escape the troubles of their life. Some sing, some dance, some even turn to drugs. Nancy sewed. Didn't matter what – clothes, bedsheets, even skirts for her daughter's Barbies, she just did it.

So, once she had left Kaylee downstairs to play with her toys, she retreated to the silence of the study to work on a quilt she had begun before the whole ordeal had started. It was nice to finally return to some resemblance of normality.

Henry was at work. Kaylee was playing. Nancy was sewing.

It was as it should be.

Then it occurred to her.

This silence. Kaylee had been quiet for an awfully long time…

Normally, there would be some background noise of Kaylee's voice, acting out some kind of bickering between her dolls. Or at least the sound of her walking around, knocking into various ornaments.

But nothing.

Absolutely nothing.

She turned her head, peering over her shoulder into the darkness of the hallway. Despite it being the middle of a sunny day, the hallway was always dressed in darkness; a lack of windows was the only thing that had originally put her and Henry off buying this house.

She listened.

Not even a murmur.

"Kaylee?" she called out, then remained still as she waited for an answer.

There was no reply.

Maybe she hadn't heard her.

"Kaylee, are you there?" she shouted once more, this time a little louder.

Impeccable silence drifted up the stairs and flooded into the room with a succinct absence.

She shuddered. Not entirely sure why this was so disturbing.

Kaylee was allowed to be quiet if she wanted to.

It was all just so...

Unusual.

Nancy placed her sewing upon the desk and wandered into the hallway. She looked back and forth, scanning every corner and crevasse of the house; not entirely sure why.

It was her daughter, for God's sake.

She needed to stop thinking there was something wrong when there wasn't.

Pausing at the top of the stairs, she strained to listen. The living room was opposite the bottom step, so any hustle or slight movement would carry, and Nancy could take it as a surety that Kaylee was safe.

But the only thing that carried up the stairs was silence and dust clouds.

The creak of the step as Nancy placed her first foot down

was far louder than it normally was, but this may have been because quiet noises always sound louder in silence.

Nancy reached the bottom step and cautiously thumped the worn-out carpet of the hallway. The open door to the living room displayed an empty presence.

Edging forward, Nancy slowly peered around the doorway, scanning the room.

A pile of dolls were left scattered across the floor, a half-empty orange juice on a cabinet, and an overwhelming emptiness encompassed the room.

This was where Nancy had left her daughter.

The windows were shut.

The front door remained locked behind her.

Where was she?

Nancy slowly rotated and took a few small steps back into the hallway and toward the kitchen. The only other room Kaylee could be in.

She tiptoed warily, keeping her eyes glued on the vacant entrance.

Why am I tiptoeing?

She shook her head to herself. Why was she so worried?

It was her daughter she was looking for.

Not some monster.

It was her nine-year-old daughter.

But, as she approached the doorway, an overwhelming chill sent itself coursing through Nancy's body; first through her bones, seizing her muscles, and inflating her lungs.

She peered around the doorway.

She nearly jumped out of her skin.

Kaylee sat at the kitchen table.

Why am I jumping? It's Kaylee...

There was something about the way Kaylee had propped herself up.

There was nothing casual in the way Kaylee was sat. It

wasn't like she was in the middle of an activity, or even in the middle of a thought. She sat at the table, her hands laid down upon the wooden surface with symmetrical precision as she stared back at Nancy with wide eyes and a wide grin.

"Hello, Mummy," Kaylee sang out.

Kaylee never calls me Mummy. It's always 'mum' or nothing.

Nancy's breath caught in her throat.

What was going on? Why was her daughter so different, and why was it freaking her out so much?

Nancy withdrew for a moment, backing up into the hallway.

She paused. Gathered herself. Shook herself back to earth.

It was her daughter. Just her daughter, but a little... off. Unwell. Unusual.

Get a grip, Nancy.

Be strong for my family.

It wasn't unusual for young children to change their dialect. Perhaps she'd heard 'mummy' somewhere else? A television program, or at school perhaps.

Once she had composed herself, shaken her mind back to normality, she returned to the kitchen.

And froze.

What the hell...

The glasses in the cabinet, through the glass door... they were upside down.

The chairs were balanced upside down on the table.

The cereal boxes along the kitchen side.

The kettle.

The handwash.

The egg timer, with its sand rushing wildly downwards.

Every single thing in this room was upside down, except for Kaylee, the chair in which she sat, and the table she rested her arms upon.

And Kaylee was in the exact same position.

Her arms hadn't moved an inch. Her smile was the same, her eyes were the same, and her unfaltering stare remained eerily on Nancy's.

Nancy's eyes scanned back and forth in disbelief.

She had been out of the room for seconds.

She hadn't heard anything but sickening silence.

Chairs, when they had touched the table... surely they would have made some noise. The glasses, to all be turned on their heads at that speed, would have created at least a gentle thudding sound as they were placed downwards.

Being able to precariously balance the kettle on its head.

How...

"Hi Mummy," Kaylee repeated.

"How..." Nancy muttered. "How did you do this?"

"Do what, Mummy?"

Nancy flinched at the way Kaylee said *Mummy*. It was with such a happy bounce, such pride. But not pride at Nancy being her mummy; pride at the kick in the teeth it gave to Nancy that she called her such a name.

"The objects... how did you do this?"

Kaylee showed the first utterance of movement she had shown since Nancy had entered the room. Keeping her body in the exact same position, Kaylee's head turned robotically to the left, then to the right, then resumed her stare.

Nancy awaited an answer.

Kaylee just kept smiling.

Kept smiling that sinister, sordid, sacrilegious smile.

"Who are you..." Nancy whispered, quiet enough that only she could hear it.

"What's the matter, Mummy?"

"I... I'm going to go lie down."

Nancy glanced once more at the room.

Her eyes were not deceiving her. It was a painting of perfectly balanced rotation, everything on its head but Kaylee.

Kaylee was such a sweet, kind girl. A friendly girl who loved her mother.

This was not her Kaylee.

APRIL'S WORDS SPUN AROUND OSCAR'S MIND LIKE A HAMSTER ON a wheel.

Julian had turned to her and announced, "We need to visit, there are things we need to clarify."

"Where is it?" April replied.

"It's in Loughborough. It's around a hundred-mile drive."

April had turned to Oscar with a sexy glint in her eye, a cheeky half-smirk, and announced:

"Let's take Oscar. See if he's ready for the big time."

So there he was. In the back of the car heading up the M42, watching Julian and April having a quiet conversation between them in the front. It took him back to being a kid, an only child stuck in the back, whilst his parents had grown-up conversations in the front that he wasn't privy to.

He ruminated on April's sassy grin and declaration that they should take Oscar. He'd found himself really wanting to impress her, somehow wanting to justify her belief in him. So that she could eventually announce, "Yes, we were right, he *is* ready for the big time!"

Maybe it was because he was lonely. Maybe it was because

it was the first girl he had ever met who gave him an ounce of attention. Or maybe it was just because it was something different that could take him away from the monotony of life.

Tewkesbury wasn't the most exciting place. It was advertised as 'a historic riverside town.' They were close.

History – yes. Everything was old and crumbling down, including the majority of its inhabitants.

Riverside – yes. There was a small river.

Town – well, there was a WHSmith. And a pharmacy. And enough charity shops to make you suspect they were taking over the world.

But as for activities, it hadn't been a particularly thriving place to grow up in, or dwell with his parents.

But now – ghosts, exorcists, demons possessing people; and he had these crazy powers that could do something about it.

Even if all this excursion was accomplishing, was to entertain and encourage April and Julian's joint delusions, at least it meant that he was doing something. Being useful.

As they joined the slip road at junction thirteen, entering a roundabout, Julian peering at his satnav, an overwhelming sense of doom overtook Oscar.

His muscles tensed, his bones stiffened, and his armpits began perspiring.

What was going on?

What was this feeling?

He abruptly choked. His lungs expanded, but it felt like no oxygen was filling them. He was wheezing, coughing, spewing up vague air from his sore throat.

Fear had taken him over.

A certainty that he was going to die overcame his immediate thoughts.

What was going on?

Why?

How?

He reached into his pocket, grasping a packet of pills, and held them out in his hands. He struggled to pop any out, such was the shaking of his hands.

After missing a few times, he finally managed to burst some medication into his palm.

He lifted the pills to his mouth.

April's hand clamped tightly around his arm.

The pills hovered away from his gaping lips, unable to cure his anxiety due to the rigid hand firmly placed around his wrist.

"What are you doing?" Oscar frantically cried.

He was starting to well up, and he really didn't want to cry in front of these people. They would think he was sad, or pathetic, or a loser.

Please don't cry.

But his arms shook, his legs seized, and his neck stiffened.

Every piece of him was consumed with a colossal need to take these pills.

He pulled at his arm, reaching his mouth forward, gaping for the release of his medication.

"Don't!" April barked.

"What?" Oscar wept. "Why?"

"Because you don't need them!"

Don't need them?

Fucking look at me!

"Yes, I do!" Oscar blubbered, reaching his jaw forward as April pulled his arm further away.

"No, you don't!" April insisted. "These feelings are not anxiety, not mental health issues, none of that. These feelings are your gift, having been suppressed for so long."

Before his eyes, a sudden premonition appeared. Of a house. A tranquil, serene, family home. A father. A mother.

A daughter.

The daughter he saw.

Kaylee.

She was laughing. Cackling, even. Sadistic roars of humour.

The girl.

The family was in trouble.

His shaking increased.

"I'm going to collapse, I need them!"

"No. You. Don't!"

April's insistent eyes reached out to him, boring into him, devouring him with her determination.

"Do not suppress your gift," she instructed. "Do not numb it. Embrace it. See what it will tell us."

April jarred his arm and the pills flew into the side of the seats and the crevices of the car's floor.

"No!" Oscar jolted upright.

Then the vision of the daughter left him.

He relaxed.

His muscles calmed, his breathing slowed, and his mind became an ecstasy of tranquillity.

"What did you see?" April asked.

"The family... the girl... they are in trouble."

April glanced at Julian, who grinned back.

"See," April smiled sincerely. "Your gift is of use."

As he stepped out of the car, Oscar's mouth dropped in awe.

It wasn't that the house itself was particularly impressive. It was your standard middle-class-family house; two floors, probably three bedrooms, nice brick, generously sized drive. Beside it was a collection of trees, with a lake just about visible beyond them.

It was the feeling in the pit of Oscar's stomach that perturbed him. A stabbing feeling, as if he had swallowed a hundred knives and they were now swirling around inside his stomach, poking rashly at each and every component of his body.

Something was wrong with this house.

Or with something within it.

"Shall we?" Julian prompted, grabbing a leather bag and marching up the porch. Oscar noticed the edge of a cross poking out of this bag, which struck him as being eerily old-fashioned.

"Come on," April prompted, and Oscar scuttled behind them to the front door.

The sound of Julian and April greeting Nancy Kemple occurred in the background, as if it was on a television with a low volume. Oscar was concentrating on other things. Like the walls.

The hallway was decorated with a light-green coating of paint, leading to a circular flower pattern on the wallpaper in the living room. Flashes of red appeared splashed against the walls, then went, like a hazy static.

A sucker punch landed into his gut, a hard hit of wind that came from nothing, and he fell to the floor.

When he lifted his head once more, the room had faded to black-and-white. He was the only one in it.

Whilst the room was modestly furnished and vacant of any person, there was something in the background. Some kind of screaming, or shouting, or moaning.

Before Oscar could find the source of the sound, he had sunk through the floorboards. In an instant, his arms disappeared and his whole body sank through the wood like quicksand, and he fell upon a solid stone floor.

Clouds of dust floated around him and, even though he had hit a hard surface with excessive velocity, he felt nothing.

The stabbing pain inside him remained, but there was no pain caused by his falling through the floorboards, and into what looked like a basement.

He laid out on his front, slowly lifting his head. The basement was consumed by shadows, coated in darkness except for a single light bulb flickering softly above him.

In the shadows, something moved.

He couldn't make out what it was.

But it was everywhere.

Encompassing the edges of the entire room, up against the walls, cloaked in the protection of the light's absence.

Crying. There was crying.

Oscar squinted.

There was movement. They were bodies. Children.

Lots of them. In rags. Cowering. Covering their heads, shielding themselves.

Oscar rose to his knees, looking to his left, to his right, and over his shoulder. They surrounded him, filling the shadows.

"What's going on?" he whispered, barely audible.

Despite the silence of his whimper, the cowering children all gasped at the sound of his voice.

So he spoke louder.

"Who are you?" he forced, trying to sound assertive, despite his voice breaking in the middle of the sentence.

Whispers echoed him, "Who are you?" being quietly gasped around the room.

"Why are you all here? What is going on?"

One of the children stepped forward, allowing a fraction of light upon her face. This girl's face revealed a deadly, charred burn up her cheek and a pattern of red scratches along the other.

"Oh, God." Oscar flinched away. "Who did this to you?"

The girl looked upwards.

"She did…" she whispered in a timid cry.

"Who's she?"

The girl lowered her head back down, focussing her eyes on Oscar's.

"The girl. She's not who she says she is."

"Which girl? Who is she?"

The child cowered. Another child stepped forward, taking her place. This time a boy, half-stripped, with scars from whiplashes spread across his chest, and a deep wound spread upon his face.

"The young girl who lives here is not that girl," the boy told Oscar.

"Then who is she?"

The boy's eyes searched back and forth, trying to summon the others; but they just cowered further into the shadows.

"She is her," the boy said.

"Her? That doesn't make any sense."

"The one who tortures us. The one who keeps us enslaved."

"The girl is keeping you enslaved?" Oscar repeated, filled with confusion.

"Please... help us..."

An unprecedented bolt jolted through Oscar's body, sending him to the floor, his head smacking against the ground.

This time he felt it.

Only, when he lifted his head, he wasn't in the basement anymore.

He was in the living room.

Everyone was staring.

Henry and Kaylee's wide eyes fixed upon him. Julian watched, intrigued. April knelt by his side, rubbing his back.

"It's okay, Oscar," April assured him.

But it wasn't okay.

Oscar was far from okay.

"Oscar, just calm down, tell us what you saw."

With complete disregard for April, he flung himself to his feet and attempted to charge at the front door. He found himself unable to balance and collapsed against the nearest wall.

Doing all he could to gain his balance, he forced himself back to his feet.

He felt someone's arms around him, trying to help, but he reached out and shoved them off him.

He didn't want help.

He didn't want anyone to touch him.

What the fuck just happened?

Using the door to steady himself, he dragged his feet to the front door and burst out, stumbling onto the lawn.

The sun shone down on him, casting burning rays over his skin, initially blinding him as he dove to the floor, shielding his eyes.

He vomited over a patch of flowers.

19

THE WORLD SPUN LIKE HE WAS DRUNK.

Oscar was on his knees, coughing up that morning's cereal, squinting with pain as his stomach churned, overcome with a painful acidic stab. Any time he tried to look up he'd stay rigidly still, but the lawn would spin to his right, the same patch of grass moving around and around and around.

"Cool it, Oscar," he heard April's voice instruct him.

Cool it?

If she wasn't so fricking hot, I'd have told her to piss off.

He felt her gentle hand rest against his back.

"Don't worry, this will go within a minute," she reassured him, though he didn't quite believe her. "You've just got to control it."

"Control it?" he gasped between sweaty panting and spits of sickly remains. "Are you fucking kidding me?"

"Oscar, man, this is something we're used to seeing in people like you."

"People like me?" he barked. "There is no 'people like me.'"

He closed his eyes for a moment. When he opened them the world still spun, but at a faster pace. April's raised eyebrow came into focus, and he seethed at her as she knelt beside him with a sympathetic smile.

"I have mental health problems," Oscar snapped. "I need my medication. This is what happens when I don't have my medication."

"And what is this, Oscar?" April laughed with a cocky smile that only infuriated Oscar further.

"This?" he echoed, with such tension it came out at a far higher pitch than he'd intended. "This is an episode."

"An episode, huh?" April chuckled.

"Would you stop laughing at me!" Oscar demanded. He tried to get to his feet but found himself unsteady, and fell straight back onto his backside.

"Relax, Oscar."

Oscar's head still pounded, but his vision was finally returning to normal. The front garden became still. Whatever it was, it had ended; but he still felt terrible.

"Would you stop telling me to relax!"

April took a bottle of water from beside her and offered it out to Oscar. She looked at him like you would a child who had gotten something wrong and had just learnt they were being silly. Her eyebrows were raised and her smile was patronisingly wide.

Oscar snatched the water bottle from her and gulped it down, not realising how dehydrated he had become.

"What did you see?" April inquired.

"What do you mean, what did I see?" Oscar frowned, taking another swig from the bottle. "What does it matter, what I saw?"

April let out a big sigh, an exhalation of irritation.

"I'm only just starting to come around to you, Oscar; don't do my nut in now."

"I do *your* nut in?"

April gazed up at the warm family home, casting her eyes over the loving house of terror.

"Inside that house," she began, "is a mother, a father, and a daughter who are going through something nothing short of atrocious. And it is our duty to help them."

"Our duty?" Oscar sneered. "What do you mean our duty? Why is it *our duty?*"

"Because we can, you fool," she joked, placing a reassuring hand on Oscar's shoulder that made him feel all warm inside.

"I can't help anyone." Oscar's eyes dropped to the floor as he despondently shook his head.

"Stop it with the puppy dog eyes and the weak boy act, it's getting old. What you had is called a *glimpse.*"

"A what?" Oscar lifted his head slightly, hesitantly intrigued.

"A glimpse, Oscar. It's what we call it when you have a vision, when you see something that isn't there, or was there, or will be there."

"What?"

"Many people have had many glimpses. A lot of them don't even know it. And if you truly have the gift, that won't be your last."

"What?!" Oscar screeched.

It was not a pleasant experience. In fact, it was a bloody awful experience, one that Oscar was happy to be medicated for and would thoroughly love to never have again.

"Don't worry," April reassured him. "Once you learn to control them, and harness them, they won't be like that. You just have to get used to them."

"I don't–"

"I have glimpses, too," April interrupted. "Well, kind of glimpses. I don't have fully formed visions like you seem to. I am able to act as a conduit for speaking to the dead, or to the beyond, and I can see visions of their life when I do it."

"Really?"

"Yes. You can see glimpses but, what Julian and I are thinking, is that your glimpses are about people, and the forces hovering around them or controlling them. You can see and feel these entities."

Oscar took a moment for this situation to sink in.

Yesterday, he was a Morrison's checkout boy.

Now I don't have a clue what is going on.

"Which is why you are important to us." She looked him dead in the eyes. "Which is why you are important to me."

He filled with a giddy buzz that sent tingles to the tips of his fingers and the tips of his toes.

"Now, what did you see?" she asked.

"I was in the basement, and there were all these children. And they were, like, I don't know..." He strained to remember, but in a sudden wave, it all came flooding back. "They said the girl is not who she says she is."

"That confirms it then."

"Confirms what?"

"The girl is not who she says she is. That, matched with the demon you saw, I'd say means we have a pretty strong case of possession."

April sprang to her feet and offered her hand out to Oscar.

"Come on, we need to help Julian do his thing."

Oscar didn't want to get up, but the simple act of being able to put his hand in hers, even if it was just to help him stand, was too inviting.

"Can I be honest?" Oscar asked, his hands tentatively twitching.

"Always," April replied.

"I still don't really buy it. I mean, I know you believe it's true, it's just... I'm an atheist. I don't believe in all this. It makes a lot more sense to me that everyone involved is crazy."

"Good," April declared. "If you believed everything, you

would be no good at this job. You need to have a sceptical mind."

She grabbed hold of his hand, which once again made his whole body tickle with teasing excitement.

"Once you have seen Julian do his thing you will believe," she asserted. "I mean, he's going to poke and prod to try and bring this demon out into the open, just to make sure. Once you've seen that happen – there is *no* questioning anything *ever again.*"

And with that, she dragged him back into the house and shut the door behind them.

20

Oscar took each creaky step with a curious hesitancy. Part of him was starting to believe, but part of him was also wary about what Julian might do to provoke this demon into revealing itself.

Yes, he could be about to witness the evidence he longed for.

But he could also be about to witness a huge case of child abuse.

Either way, he found his feet unintentionally guiding him toward the bedroom. His lip quivered as April turned back to him and gave him a deep, sincere gaze into his eyes.

"Are you ready for this?" she asked.

Oscar reluctantly nodded.

"Remember – a demon will say and do things to provoke you, and everyone else in the room. You must not respond to it, or listen to it. You understand?"

He nodded once more.

"Oscar, I'm going to need an actual confirmation from you that you understand this."

"Y-yes," he stuttered. "I understand."

"Julian is going to get this thing to say its name. If it admits to being Ardat Lili, or Lilith – we will take that as evidence."

Bracing herself with a deep breath and relaxing her muscles, they entered the bedroom.

As Oscar passed the threshold he was hit with a sudden stab of frozen air. His breath was visible, such was the low temperature of the room. Henry stood in the corner of the room with a tearful Nancy in his arms, shielding her from the potential torment.

Julian stood dominantly over the bed, over Kaylee, whose wrists were fastened to the bed-posts with handcuffs, and her ankles with belts. The girl looked distraught; a face full of fear, tears trickling down her cheeks, no understanding of what was happening.

A sickening feeling of uncertainty filled Oscar. This wasn't right. It felt like a scene from a movie, one that would never realistically happen due to the complete negligence and disregard for the child involved. This child didn't look possessed; she looked devastated. Utterly inconsolable at what her parents and these strangers were doing to her.

"Are we ready?" Julian prompted April with a deadened voice. April nodded and shut the door behind them.

Julian turned to Kaylee on the bed beneath him, glaring at her with a face full of disdain.

This wasn't right.

Whatever these people believed, Oscar couldn't watch this.

This is just wrong.

"April, I can't–" he began, but was abruptly silenced as April shushed him.

Julian made the shape of a cross over his body, then kissed his hands. He dropped his head, closing his eyes, and giving a silent prayer. When his eyes shot open they were full of determined resolution. Full of tenacity; they were the eyes of a man with strong convictions in what he was about to do.

"Kaylee, are you okay?" Julian asked.

The little girl turned her head, eyes full of tears, and gaped wide-eyed at the scary man stood over her.

"Listen to me, Kaylee," Julian began. "I know this is tough, and I know you don't want to do this, but I'm going to need to speak to whatever it is inside you."

She vigorously shook her head, tears streaming down her face, pleading under her breath, "No, no, no, please, no…"

"I need you to be strong," Julian insisted. "If you want us to get this thing out of you, I need you to be really, really strong."

"Please…" she begged, her voice jittering like a scratched disc.

"Just relax, take a back seat, and let us talk to this thing. Can you do that for us? Can you be strong?"

Kaylee briefly closed her eyes and heavily exhaled. She feebly nodded. Her tensed muscles relaxed. Her whole body sank into the bed.

"I am no longer speaking to Kaylee. I speak to the thing within. In the name of God, I command you to reveal yourself."

Kaylee remained still, her eyes staring at the ceiling above, bloodshot and unmoved.

"In the name of the Father, the Son, and the Holy Ghost, I implore you, demon, reveal to us your name."

Oscar backed up against the wall. He glanced at the parents in the corner of the room, the mother with her face plastered against her husband's chest, unable to watch.

"In Jesus' name, I require you to reveal yourself!"

"Why are you doing this?" Kaylee whimpered, a small, weak voice echoing from her shaking body.

"What is your name?"

Kaylee locked eyes with Oscar.

"Why are you letting them do this to me?" she asked. "Why aren't you stopping them?"

Oscar gazed back, mortified, pinned against the wall.

Why was Oscar letting them do this?

Why wasn't Oscar stopping them?

"April, get me my bag," Julian commanded.

April picked up the tatty, leather bag and took it over to Julian. He withdrew a cross, gently kissed it, and dropped the bag to the floor.

"In the name of the holy angels and archangels, reveal your name."

"Please, stop them!" Kaylee continued to beseech Oscar. "Why won't you stop them?"

Julian grabbed the cross and pressed it up against the young girl's chest. She writhed in pain, struggling under the pressure Julian was putting on her with his wooden weapon.

"Please, make it stop!" the girl moaned. "Why are you hurting me?"

Oscar shook his head. This was assault. This was cruelty. He couldn't do this.

Julian lifted the cross to Kaylee's neck and pressed down hard, and harder still.

"Please!" Kaylee lifted her head back but kept her eyes hell-bent on Oscar's. "Please do something!"

Julian pressed the cross again on her neck so hard she stopped breathing. Beneath his firm grip she suffocated, coughing and choking against him – but Julian did not repent.

"You need to stop this," Oscar spoke, so softly no one noticed.

"I can't breathe!" the girl cried, then squinted a glare toward Oscar. "You really are a shitty little loser, aren't you?" she asked mockingly.

She gasped for air that didn't come.

Oscar couldn't take this anymore.

He couldn't be a witness to this.

He couldn't stand by and watch a child die.

Without a moment's hesitation, he burst out of the room and marched down the corridor.

"Where are you going?" demanded April's voice. Oscar froze and turned to see her standing in the doorway of the bedroom.

"This is barbaric!" Oscar claimed.

"Are you fucking kidding me?" April growled, full of aggression Oscar had never seen from her before.

"He's throttling her!"

"He's throttling the demon!"

Oscar turned and strode to the stairs.

"She's right, isn't she?" April asked with a mocking shake of the head.

"What?" Oscar asked, pausing on the top step.

"What Kaylee just said. What the demon just said. You are a shitty little loser."

Oscar shook his head, full of adamant resistance.

"You can't hold that against me," he retorted. "Just because I'm not going to watch a child be tortured."

"You really think a child suffocating would say to a random person in the room that they are a loser, huh?"

Oscar went to reply but had nothing. She was right.

"I'm not going to keep chasing you!" April was shouting now, full of anger, full of frustration. "If every time things get a little rough, if every time you feel it's too stressful, you bail, then go on. Fuck off. We don't need you."

Oscar looked to his feet, shaking his head.

All his life.

All his life, he had run.

"Make the choice, Oscar. Either you're going to man up and help us, or you are going to leave now and never look back. Either way, choose. Because I can't be arsed with you running off no more."

With that, she went back into the room and slammed the door behind her.

Oscar lingered on that top step.

Thinking deeply.

There was something going on here.

Was he going to admit it? Face it? Fight it?

Or was he going to do what he had always done?

With a reluctant sigh, and a brief moment of contemplation, he found his feet carrying him straight back into that room.

With an approving nod from April, he looked to Julian doing all he could to pin down Kaylee, who was bouncing and seizing, pulling against her restraints.

"Grab her legs!" Julian shouted at Oscar. Oscar didn't waste a moment in complying, grabbing hold of Kaylee's legs and pinning them down, just as April forced down her waist and Julian pinned down her shoulders.

Oscar saw the girl's eyes. They had changed.

They were something else.

Her pupils had fully dilated, with trails of red spiralling in every direction.

Her body rose fractionally off the bed, stiff as a plank.

It laughed, but this laugh was deep, croaky, sinister. Not the kind of voice a little girl would speak.

"For the last time, demon," Julian spoke, clearly and succinctly. "What is your name?"

Kaylee moved her head toward Julian – or rather, the demon moved Kaylee's head toward Julian. Looking him deep in his eyes, Oscar watched her grin grow, witnessing what he thought he would never witness.

"My name is Ardat Lili," it croaked, full of triumphant arrogance. "But you can call me Lilith."

Jason understood why some officers never married.

It was gone 2.00 a.m.

Five hours since his shift had ended.

And there he was. Sat half-shaven, half-awake, with a half-empty paper cup perched on his crotch – his ninth coffee that day.

What was worse, he saw nothing wrong with that.

And he knew his wife would be furious.

It was just… that girl. Something about her was off. At first, it was a trivial curiosity. Since getting hold of the CCTV footage of her interview and playing it over and over, it had become an incessant nagging. A need to understand. Call it the instinct of experience, or call it being a nosy, lifeless prick; it just didn't make any sense.

He rewound the stream and watched Kaylee Kemple once more.

Still, she sat there. Motionless. A sadistic grin.

Yes, it was extreme to call the smile of a nine-year-old girl 'sadistic.' How could a girl that age have any kind of evil temperament? Personality disorders, or even psychopathy, were known to develop in late adolescence. It was just something...

Off.

That was the only way he could describe it, and it was immensely frustrating. Almost twenty years into the job and the best he could come up with was, "She's off."

"Pathetic," he muttered to himself, finishing the last of his cold, grainy coffee he couldn't even remember making.

The girl was from a middle-class family. Her dad was a doctor. Her mother was an incredibly caring woman. There were no nurturing influences to create negative behaviour.

So, what was it?

He crumpled the paper cup and threw it at the bin, missing completely and hitting the wall. Slamming his fist on the table with a heavy hand, he leant forward in his chair, getting as close to the screen as possible.

He rubbed his eyes, shook his head and ran his hands through his hair, doing whatever he could to wake himself up.

His next shift started in a few hours.

May as well just sleep in his office chair. It wouldn't be the first time.

His eyes hovered inches from the screen, staring avidly at the pixelated face.

She didn't blink.

Not once did the damn girl blink.

She stared back at the questioning officer, eyes wide open, a smile spread across her cute little cheeks. Freckles gleaming on a face full of guilty innocence, a mocking smile mocking the useless interrogation.

"My daddy molested me," she would repeat every now and then. It was like she was stuck on repeat. A toy doll that could only say one thing.

And the way she said it... It was so bouncy, so playful. It

was like she was saying, "I'd like a lolly," or, "Would you like to play with me?"

Her hands remained at perfect symmetry to each other at all times, resting on each knee. She wore a spotty t-shirt and a frilly skirt. The skirt rode up her legs, as if intentionally. She sat with legs wide open, a playful glint in her eyes filled with lust.

Which was ridiculous to think. Perverted, even.

It's a nine-year-old girl, for Christ's sake.

He'd met many women who attempted to use their sexuality to distract the man questioning them. Particularly hookers guilty of drugs or theft.

But to accuse a young girl – a *child* – of doing it was preposterous.

Yet, there was something remotely lecherous in the way she sat, peering at the man looking toward her.

There were some ridiculous theories floating around that this girl was possessed.

Maybe.

"Jesus," he growled at himself, leaning back in his chair.

What was wrong with him? Accusing a little girl of not only trying to seduce an officer but being possessed.

It really was time to go home.

His bed was calling him, home to what was likely an angry wife.

As was his half-empty bottle of whiskey stood solitary on his desk.

A dirty tumbler glass waiting to be filled and weakly sipped.

Yet, despite willing himself to get up, get his coat, and get going, he couldn't. He felt compelled to keep watching. Keep thinking. Find the answer.

He paused the video.

And froze.

"What the fuck…"

This time he knew he should go home and go to bed.

Because at the exact moment he had paused it…

On the frozen screen in front of him…

The innocent little girl's eyes flickered red, and a contorted shadow spread across the wall behind her.

2 2

THE STARS HUNG GRACEFULLY IN THE STILL NIGHT SKY. THE SUN had long since set, and the tranquillity of the restful dark painted the night sky with harmony.

A run-down hotel stood loosely beside an empty car park. Cars could be heard speeding across the nearby motorway, and the 'o' sign for 'hotel' flickered erratically.

Inside a busy hotel room, April lay casually on the bed. Oscar perched on the end, watching Julian, who paced back and forth agitatedly. Julian continually muttered to himself, and Oscar could only just pick out odd snippets such as, "No no no," "Think, damn it," and, "Why her?"

Oscar glanced over his shoulder at April, who simply played on her phone, not paying any attention. She was evidently used to Julian's frantic pacing back and forth, and Oscar could imagine it being a frequent occurrence whilst they were in the midst of an investigation.

Oscar still couldn't entirely believe what had happened. Had he really seen a girl levitate? How had her eyes become red? And how did she make such an impossibly low-pitched noise?

No longer did he feel foolish in admitting that he was beginning to believe what they were telling him.

"Right!" Julian abruptly declared. "I've got it."

April put her phone away and listened, prompting Oscar to also pay attention.

"I am going to make a phone call to grant consent for an exorcism," he decided. "Then – I am going to bed."

Without a moment's hesitation, he marched out the door and his footsteps grew faint as they disappeared down the corridor.

Oscar turned to April, slightly bemused. An instant decision for quite an extreme solution – an exorcism – then bolting out the door to sleep.

"Don't worry about it," April reassured him, as if reading his mind. "You'll get used to his erratic ways."

"What's his deal?" Oscar asked, turning himself around so he was sitting cross-legged on the bed, leaning comfortably towards April. "I mean, he seems quite intense."

"Yeah, he can be. But he's good at what he does."

Oscar nodded, giving a slight chuckle.

April leant forward, echoing Oscar's body language. His whole body shook. They were so close he could see the various shades of red on her lip. Her welcoming scent clung to the air around him, filling his belly with fluttering butterflies. Her eyes were focussed on his; her wide, big, blue eyes.

"So, Oscar," she began, putting her hands on his legs in a friendly gesture that shot through him in a lightning strike of lust. "What's your deal?"

"What do you mean?" he asked faintly, full of nerves.

"What's your family?"

"Well, I have a mum, a dad, a cat… that's pretty much it. No brothers or sisters or anything."

"What are your mum and dad like?"

"Well, she's horrible, but I think that's just because I've let them down...." He thought about it for a few moments. "They used to be amazing. Supportive, loving. Best I could hope for." He dropped his head. "More than I deserve, I guess. I... I've been a bit of a let-down. I don't know, I just never really had much ambition."

Oscar stopped himself talking, as he realised how much unprompted information he was giving. She didn't need to know this. Why would she even care?

It was at this point he realised just how lonely he was. The first point of human contact and he was spilling his guts. First time being this close to a female, and he was sat there with his hormones raging.

"So I guess working at Morrison's your entire life isn't really your ambition?"

Oscar chuckled.

"No."

"Well, now you're a Sensitive. You'll never have to work there again."

Lifting his head with a genuine smile, he thought about what that would be like. Working with April, day after day, solving people's ghostly problems. It was a dream.

"What about you?" Oscar prompted. "What's your, like, powers?"

"My *gift*," she began, stressing the world gift, "is that I can act as a conduit. I can sense that not of this world, in a similar way to how you can see it."

"What's a conduit?"

"A conduit," she began, edging closer still, smiling at him, "is someone who acts as, like, an empty house, for someone from the other side to stay in when we need to talk."

"So, you have, like, demons and stuff inside of you?"

"In a way, yes."

"What's that like?"

"I don't know, I kind of take a back seat when it happens. They take the house, and I go sit in the garden."

She laughed at her ridiculous analogy. Her laughter was heavenly, a joyous sound Oscar could listen to all day.

"What about your parents, your family?" Oscar asked.

Then the smile went.

Her whole face changed. Her eyes briefly lingered on his, then looked away. Her smile faded to a frown and she anxiously bit her lip. Her body that had only moments before been leant toward him in an upright position, entering his personal space, was now hunched over. Her hands ran over her arms, warming them.

She stood, meandering to the window, away from Oscar. Away from the perfect situation they had just shared.

"I'm sorry, April, I–"

"We have a long day tomorrow," she interrupted. "You should go to your room. Go to sleep."

She didn't avert her solemn gaze from the window. She looked so lonely, a solitary being in need of love.

But Oscar didn't know how to give that to her. It wasn't like he was particularly experienced with girls. It wasn't like he knew how to break down someone's defences and get through to them, to beseech them to share their deepest, darkest secrets, to reveal their ghosts.

So he stood, looked at her one more time, and turned. Shoving his hands in his pockets, and ruing himself for ruining such a perfect moment, he left the room.

Shortly after, he crawled into bed in the room next door.

Though he was sure he could hear a faint sobbing from the other side of the wall.

HUMIDITY HUNG IN THE MORNING AIR. A SOFT BREEZE accompanied, but did little to quell the heat.

Oscar didn't mind. This was how he liked it. Warm.

He couldn't stand the cold.

Glancing at his watch, he willed April to hurry up. He was stood beside the car with Julian in awkward silence.

Julian didn't seem perturbed by it. He stood casually, smoothly leant against his car with an air of patience. Like waiting for April was something he was used to.

Oscar was not so relaxed. He shifted his weight from one foot to the other, his legs growing increasingly tired from standing still. He occasionally glanced at Julian but tried not to stare, in fear that Julian would reciprocate his glance and the situation would grow even more uncomfortable.

"Relax," Julian eventually spoke. "You're wasting energy."

Oscar tried to stand still. He would get in the car, but it was too hot to even touch. The metal rims and the car seat needed cooling, and the air conditioning seemed to be doing little about it.

"So…" Oscar attempted, deciding to break the silence. "How long have you known April?"

Julian looked to Oscar with an expression full of irritation. As if he was perturbed to be having his thoughts disrupted by meaningless chatter.

"A while."

"Oh, yeah?" Oscar nodded, trying to think of another question to ask but coming up short.

"Why do you ask?" Julian blankly prompted, his eyes squinting sceptically toward Oscar like he was a mugger asking for the time.

"I don't know, just wondered."

"You're not growing an extra fondness for our April, are you?" Julian folded his arms and raised his eyebrows.

Oscar couldn't lie. He was an awful liar.

"Well, yeah, she's all right, I guess. She's cool. I like her."

Julian took a moment to survey the nearby surroundings, then turned his face to Oscar, focussing dead on his eyes.

"If you so much as touch her, I'll break your legs."

Oscar froze.

Did he just hear that right?

His hands twitched clumsily. An inept stuttering bounced out of his quivering lips.

"What?" Oscar asked, attempting to sound big and confident, but only coming out as a whisper.

"You heard," Julian replied. "I've been with April for years."

"You mean, you're *with* her?"

"No, you dope. As in, we've been doing this for years. I picked her up off the streets when she was fifteen."

Oscar's jaw dropped. He did not know this.

"What happened?"

"She ran away from home at fourteen when she decided she'd rather the streets than her parents."

"Oh my God, I didn't know…"

"I found her a year later, living in a cheap sleeping bag on the porch of a broken-down shop. I could tell there was something about her. See, that's part of my gift – I can see this in others."

"She actually lived on the streets?"

"I helped April to harness her gift, to use it. I've watched her grow into the woman she is today. And I wouldn't stand by as some little dweeb undoes all that."

As if by perfect timing, April appeared from her room and sauntered over to them.

Oscar remained transfixed, rooted to the spot, staring open-mouthed at April as she strutted sexily toward them. He was attracted to her, he couldn't deny that – except, now there was something else. A new found respect. Living on the streets at fourteen.

To have overcome such things…

It was remarkable.

And to think he was complaining to her last night that his parents were too supportive, and wanted him to have ambitions.

I'm such a doofus.

"Here she is," Julian greeted her. "Did you lose your way?"

"Hardy har!" April mockingly retorted, then turned to Oscar and gave him a sneaky wink. "Mornin', squirt."

Julian and April climbed into the front of the car. Oscar had to quickly bring himself back to earth and remind himself to take his seat in the back.

Growing up on the streets? Sleeping on the porch of a broken-down shop?

He didn't take his eyes from her for the entire drive.

No wonder Julian was so protective.

24

Oscar stood alone at the back of the room, watching Julian prepare for the exorcism with a perfectionist's precision. It was like watching an obsessive doctor prepare his tools for surgery. Every item was taken out of his bag, held, meticulously contemplated, and laid out in perfect symmetry upon a table next to him.

The final three items were withdrawn with such care it was like Julian was nursing a child.

With gentle hands he lifted a pristine, leather-bound book with nothing but a gold cross indented on it, which glinted in the faint lamplight. He briefly rested it against his forehead, closing his eyes, breathing it in, then placed it perfectly upon the table beside him. He opened it to a specific section, where he ran his hand over the thin pages to ensure there were no creases.

He withdrew a small set of rosary beads. They were like an old, string necklace, with black circles decorating the length of its body. At the end was a small, silver cross. Julian wrapped the string around his right hand a few times until it was firmly in place, and lifted the cross to his mouth. He gently placed a soft, lingering kiss upon it, closing his eyes and taking a deep moment of scrutinising thought.

Following this, he placed the rosary beads around his neck and tucked them beneath his shirt.

Finally, and most mysteriously, he withdrew a picture. Oscar didn't manage to get a decent glance at this picture but was sure it was of a young woman he didn't recognise.

Julian stole a brief glance at this photo and tucked it into his inside pocket.

"Leave me," Julian instructed. "I need to say my final prayers. I will let April know when to bring the girl."

Julian's eyeline didn't falter from the empty bed and the vacant restraints beneath him. Despite giving orders, his demands were gently spoken. His eyes glazed over as if in a translucent state, within a deep, mental preparation.

Oscar complied without hesitation and left the room. He made his way down the hallway to the closed door of the child's bedroom, where April stood.

"How is he?" April asked.

"Fine, I guess," Oscar answered honestly, having no reference of comparison to know whether Julian's preparations were the norm. "Is Kaylee okay?"

"She's in there with her parents now."

Oscar held April's eye contact. They shared a moment of content silence. It felt like they were preparing for battle; as if a solemn, devastating act was about to take place. Everyone was speaking so quietly, acting so serenely. Like it was the calm before the storm.

"Julian said you'd know when to bring the girl."

"Yeah," April confirmed, nodding. "He normally needs a bit of time to prepare."

"He had a photo that he put in his pocket. What was it?"

April's head dropped. She flexed her fingers and curled her hands into fists, doing her best to mask her discomfort. After gathering her thoughts, she lifted her head and fixed her eyes on Oscar's.

"It's of a young woman," April informed him, speaking slowly and softly. An assured solemnness echoed in her voice. "It is the photograph of the first woman he ever performed an exorcism on. He was one of only around ten people the church allowed to perform an exorcism, despite not being an ordained priest. He was taught along with a few other Sensitives by a man called Derek Lansdale. I know you don't know who he is, but if you did, trust me, you'd be impressed."

"That's a bit weird though, isn't it?" Oscar mused. "I mean, why does he need to carry a photo of his first exorcism around?"

April hesitated. She pursed her lips and gave a slight, unconscious shake of the head.

"Because she died, Oscar," April finally admitted. "Julian did his best, but the girl did not survive."

"She died?" Oscar was agape. "I didn't realise someone could die in something like this!"

"Oh, yes, they definitely can. And they have. And Julian never forgets it."

Oscar was lost for words.

Julian had lost a girl to death in an exorcism...

How bad could it have been?

Surely it was just saying a few words, babbling a few prayers, a spray of holy water, and it was done?

"How..." he unintentionally gasped.

"I don't think you quite realise what is about to occur, do you, Oscar?"

"I..."

"An exorcism isn't a wham, bam, thank you ma'am kind of thing. It can take hours. Sometimes days, weeks even. You are fighting something made of pure evil. Something that doesn't give up without a fight."

"I… I don't know what to say…"

"An exorcism changes you, Oscar. Remember that."

The door behind Oscar creaked open, and Julian stepped halfway out.

"I'm ready, April," he spoke gently, and returned to the room.

With a raise of her eyebrows Oscar interpreted as a gesture of "here we go," she knocked on the door behind her.

"It's time," she announced.

A few moments passed and the door opened.

Nancy stepped out, wiping the corners of her eyes with a tissue.

Henry followed, placing an arm around his wife.

This gave Oscar a chance to look at the little girl.

But this was no little girl.

In body, yes. But her face was deathly pale, and her eyes a fully dilated mixture of black and red. Her skin was torn, dirty fingernails were cracked, and the crotch of her ripped pyjamas was stained blood red.

It focussed its eyes on Oscar and grinned a wide, sickening grin.

For the first time Oscar was absolutely, unequivocally sure that he was not in the presence of something human – but of something completely and entirely evil.

25

THERE WERE MANY BAD EXPERIENCES NANCY EXPECTED TO HAVE to endure as a mother.

The pain of watching them leave for the first day at school, for university, for a first date.

When they get bullied at school or get their heart broken for the first time and they come home to you, crying into your arms.

Mental health issues. Illnesses. Anxiety.

All terrible things, but things to be expected.

But Nancy had never expected this.

She still questioned herself. Was this the right thing to do? Or was she sanctioning child abuse on her own daughter?

She had to remind herself.

She *saw* her daughter rise off the bed.

She *heard* her daughter speak in a voice she couldn't possibly speak in.

She *felt* something in her house that had replaced the loving embrace of Kaylee.

Such a happy-go-lucky child, full of curiosity and friendliness. The kind of child who would spark a conversation with a stranger for no apparent reason.

Turned to this.

A shadow of the girl she was.

It took everything she had to hold herself back, to keep herself secluded in her husband's arms. To watch helplessly as her daughter was ripped out of her bed, kicking and screaming, and led to the cold bedroom that had been prepared for her.

She stood with Henry, watching for as long as she could.

They tied her down on the bed, fastening her arms and legs. She resisted. Kicking. Screaming. Punching. Nancy didn't know if that's what she had expected. She had no idea what she had expected.

But not this.

Not witnessing such torture.

She couldn't watch. She turned to her husband's chest and soaked his shirt with her tears. She grew repulsed at the sound of her own weeping. Loud, audible convulsions of tears, crying helplessly.

Because it's all she could do.

Cry.

It's all a mother can ever do.

Just watch as their child wanders alone into the world, hoping that they will return to you. Hoping beyond hope that they know they can.

She couldn't watch the exorcism. It was heart-wrenching.

Though she expected not watching may be just as bad. She'd experienced the noises coming from her room over the past month. The sounds were atrocious. Vile, disgusting, sickening screams, pounding against the walls, destroying their disrupted sleep.

But it was not her daughter's voice.

And she had to remember this.

It was her body, but it was not her.

The voice wailing from the jaw that loudly clicked out of place came in multiple pitches. It was low, it was high, it was croaky, it was painful – but none of it was Kaylee. Her voice was not there. Not even a resemblance of it was etched into the triumphant screams of the demon feigning pain in a ploy to play with the family who cared so much for its victim.

Some prayer was being shouted at her. She tuned it out. They were all words. The Father, the God, the Holy Ghost, all of it was just words.

If there was a god, then he let this happen to her daughter.

When she died, when she came face-to-face with this transient being – she would be having a few strong words.

Where was he?

The exorcist was calling on him to help, but where was he when the demon took her? Huh?

Where was he then?

"Nancy, I think we need to leave them to it," Henry suggested, obviously deciding her crying was getting too loud. That her emotional state was becoming a burden for others to bear.

Maybe it was disrupting what the Sensitives were trying to do.

She didn't care.

She would not leave her daughter.

"Come on, honey, we need to go. We need to leave them to it."

"No!" she cried out, resisting with all her might.

"Nancy, we can't help them like this." Henry turned to Julian, taking hold of his wife. "We'll be just outside, okay?"

He held his arms tightly around her, but she rooted her feet to the floor like two dead weights.

"I can't…" she wept.

"We have to. Come on." He lifted her chin so her red, wet

eyes could see his. "We will sit on the stairs outside. We'll be right there if she needs us. Come on."

She knew it made sense.

She stole a glance over her shoulder at her daughter.

She wailed in pain.

It wailed in pain.

Or in masochistic joy.

She couldn't bear to decide.

Feeling resolute, she allowed her husband to drag her out of the room, placing her on the top step.

She flung her arms around him and squeezed with all her might, holding on and not letting go.

WATCHING OSCAR MADE APRIL THINK BACK TO HER FIRST exorcism.

Despite being fifteen when Julian took her in, she was at least seventeen before she had truly begun to master her gift. Julian had still refused to take her to an exorcism until she was eighteen.

This had really annoyed her. How was it she was old enough to be used as a conduit, and to be exposed to this morbid, malevolent life – but she wasn't old enough to witness an exorcism?

She remembered Julian's words clearly: "A conduit is someone who lends their body to the occult. A possessed victim is a person who has had their body stolen. You are not ready to see such a lack of control."

April had seen many, many things in her life. From her sleeping bag she had watched women get harassed, men fight, and had even been pissed on by an aggressive drunk. How was it she had been exposed to such evil but wasn't deemed a capable enough witness to the removal of a demon from its victim?

She had thought it was ridiculous.

Then she witnessed her first exorcism.

And she understood the reasons in a way one never can until they experience the thing itself. She'd known little about Julian's experience of being an exorcist. She only knew vaguely of Anna, the girl he had sadly lost a few years before.

But seeing the things she saw... Hearing the things she heard... It was traumatic. But, far worse than the things she saw or heard were the personal taunts. The way each demon seemed to know every little thing about her life, and how it could use that knowledge against her.

What's worse, the demon's verbal tirade was normally bizarrely perceptive and full of painful truths.

She had since become immune. She'd managed to thicken her skin to it.

But now, watching Oscar, she recognised the look of abject fear and paralysing confusion painted across his face. The look that showed he hated having to do this but felt compelled to by some moral duty. He couldn't argue with it, couldn't deny his true calling – but hated having to listen to what the demon said.

He struggled to endure it in exactly the way April struggled to watch it.

And now, she could see Oscar's struggle to endure. And she could see the demon picking up on its advantage over him perfectly.

"Hey, you," it's wicked, deep voice croaked out of the face of a scared little girl. "Yeah, the scrawny one stood at the back who hasn't got a clue what he's doing."

Oscar glanced nervously at April, who held her hand out in a calm, reassuring manner. Some attempt to keep him cool, keep him undeterred. They couldn't let him react to it. A demon feeds off negative energy.

"You want to fuck me, don't you?" the demon taunted.

"What?" Oscar replied, a face full of horror.

"Oscar, don't," April instructed him.

The room was chaos. The window had smashed to bits and fragments of glass were dancing in a tornado of objects. The bed the girl was restrained upon rattled, bashing and banging against the floor and the wall. Its laughter never stopped. Despite how much Julian shouted and screamed his prayers its quiet, subdued laughter still stood out above the noise with an uncomfortable prominence.

"In the name of the Father, the Son, and the Holy Spirit, we demand you, demon Lilith, leave this girl!" Julian repeated his demands repeatedly until they became white noise. They didn't seem to be doing a damn thing.

"No, no, no," the demon sang in a mocking, sinister voice. "It's not me you want to fuck, is it? It's *her!*"

The demon's eyes shot to April, whose stare consequently turned to Oscar. She saw his face full of awkward distress, evidently desperate not to let such information be divulged.

"Every time she touches you, every time she looks at you, you get some big fucking hard-on, don't you?"

"Shut up!" Oscar shouted.

"No, Oscar!" April demanded, moving in front of him, blocking his view of the wretched demon, gripping his shoulders. "You can't react, you will only fuel it. Endure it."

"You like how she's touching you now, don't you? Touch his dick, I bet it's like a rock."

She could see the question written over Oscar's face – how were such words coming from a nine-year-old girl?

She had to let him suffer it. She couldn't allow him to react. He had to learn. If he was going to do this, he had to grow a thick skin to the abuse.

Only he wasn't a particularly confident, thick-skinned person.

"I bet you don't even like her. You're just lonely and pathetic."

She saw Oscar's eyes peering at the demon over her shoulder. Squinting, glaring, full of rage.

"You don't have a chance. You are a fucking nerd with a small dick and no life. You may as well just die."

"Oscar, look at me," she urged him, unsuccessfully. "Don't look at it, look at me."

"You don't have a gift," the demon persisted.

"Oscar, look at me," she pleaded.

"Your life is nothing, and you may as well not live it."

She could see him deciding that the demon was telling the truth.

She could see it winning.

His face was consumed with terror as the realisation dawned upon him that this demon was right.

But the demon wasn't right.

She needed to do something.

"You pathetic, scrawny little maggot. She hates you. Everyone does."

Tears glistened in the corner of his eyes.

Without thinking or comprehending what she was doing, she grabbed the side of his cheeks and pulled his face into hers. She planted a soft but firm kiss upon his lips, lingering for a few seconds, then pulling away, looking him deep in the eyes.

His eyes widened toward her, his open jaw shaking. He looked gleefully apprehensive yet elatedly confused.

"Now stop listening to it, and help us," she demanded.

"Guys, I need your help," Julian announced, urging them closer with the wave of his arm.

Oscar nodded firmly at April.

Together, they stepped toward the end of the bed, ready to do what they could.

27

THE HANDCUFFS SHATTERED INTO PIECES.

The ankle restraints flew off with ease.

The girl rose from the bed, the demon forcing her to helplessly levitate.

Oscar pushed down upon Kaylee's ankles with what little strength he had. Despite her being such a little girl, it felt like he was pushing against a brick wall.

He could see April across from him struggling to hold down Kaylee's arms. At least it wasn't just him who couldn't pin her down.

The girl's body lingered in the air, her crotch raised up as her arms and legs dangled beneath her like spaghetti.

Oscar gave up trying to hold her down. Not only was he competing with her immense weight, but also with the chaos of the room. The loose furniture bustled, vibrating across the floor. The window smashed in, sending tiny fragments of glass bustling in circles. The floor shook, unsteadying his shaking legs.

"Mother of God!" cried out Julian, "of blessed Michael the

Archangel, of the blessed apostles Peter and Paul and all the saints."

"Give me your fucking worst," the demon insisted, tormenting Julian with its resistance.

Oscar was impressed with how little Julian allowed this thing to faze him. Oscar's whole body convulsed with shakes of fear, flinching every time this thing spoke or settled its sickening eyes upon him. He doubted his eyes, in disbelief of what he saw, but did not doubt his nose nor the temperature; he was repulsed at the foul smell of the room and shivering from the cold. Still, Julian stood defiantly. Throughout the entire ordeal, Julian wore a disobedient snarl that he did not let up.

It was the face of experience.

"Come on, you cunt, is that it?"

"With the holy authority of God, we confidently undertake to repulse the attacks and deceits of the devil."

"I love the deceits of the devil!"

Oscar and April were flung to the floor, like an invisible cannonball had fired into their bellies, forcing them onto their backs. Oscar slammed into the far wall and April knocked into a nearby lamp.

Groaning in pain, Oscar looked over at April and saw her struggling to get up. Her hand gently dabbed a throbbing red bump on her forehead.

Oscar tried to get up and help her but found himself pushed into the wall once more, pinned down and forced to watch April as she clattered into a wardrobe door.

She did not get up.

Julian grabbed his cross, clutching it tightly, gripping it, holding it toward the demon. This seemed to help, like it was a barrier that stopped him from being thrown across the room like the other two, as he was only made to stumble backwards a few steps.

Oscar watched with a mixture of astonishment and horror

as the girl continued to rise until she was easily six feet off the ground, hanging helplessly.

"God arises, his enemies are scattered!" Julian persisted.

"I know you, Julian Barth."

Kaylee's deformed, mangled face locked eyes with Julian.

"You know who I am?"

"Smoke is driven away, as wax melts before the fire!"

"You know what I do to men when they sleep?"

"The wicked perish at the presence of God."

"Hey – how's Anna?"

If the reminder of this girl's death upset Julian, he didn't show it. He swiftly produced a small bottle with a cross engraved on it. Unscrewing it as quickly as he could, he splashed it over the floating body. Hisses of burning tinged the girl's skin, causing a wave of smoke to waft upwards. The demon plummeted back to the bumpy mattress.

"Anna says that you were the one who deserved to die."

This was a perfect time for Julian to go all-out attack, to continue his barrage of prayers and flicking his holy water.

But he didn't.

Julian had faltered. Frozen in stupefied trepidation.

His face looked locked onto what the demon had just said.

This Anna girl had affected him deeply.

But he was experienced.

He had to have enough resolve to deal with it.

With an aggressive snarl, he put bad thoughts to the back of his mind and stood strong.

But it was too late.

The demon had already taken advantage of the momentary lapse in concentration.

It dove off the bed, launched itself toward the shattered window and smashed through it, crushing the remaining pieces of glass to pieces like it was powdery ash.

Julian rushed to the window, April following. Oscar

abruptly got to his feet and joined them just in time to see the faint shadow of a girl disappear into the trees.

"Where is she going?" April asked.

Both she and Oscar watched Julian, cautiously expectant. They could not let her get away.

"The lake," Julian replied. "There's a lake through those trees."

Without a moment's hesitation, Julian sprinted out of the room, thudding past Kaylee's parents and down the stairs.

"What do we do?" Oscar asked helplessly to April.

"Whatever we can," she retorted, following Julian out of the door.

Oscar cast his eyes over the now-vacant chaos of the room, torn strips of wallpaper ripped to shreds, shards of glass ingrained in the carpet, and ripped, bloody bedsheets glistening in the moonlight.

Forcing himself forward, he charged to the door of the room and followed the steps of the others.

IT TOOK EVERY MUSCLE AND EVERY OUNCE OF ENERGY OSCAR had to keep up with the heavy rustles of April's feet treading on damp leaves. He could see her faint shadow between the trees ahead, most likely following Julian's faint shadow.

His stomach rumbled, pushing a swig of sick to his mouth.

But he needed to be strong.

He willed himself to be strong.

He spat it out and continued.

The trees became sparser and sparser until Oscar found himself coming to an opening. Before him was a peaceful lake, dimly lit beneath a generous moon, surrounded by green plants, red flowers, and other natural beauty.

A few yards down the lake, the water was not so peaceful. He could hear thrashing and shouting and deep-throated, sinister cackles. Oscar instinctively ran in the direction of the voices, stumbling over a loose branch as he lurched himself forward.

Kaylee's wounded, demented body lay scantily clad in a wooden boat, taunting the girl's saviours with greyed hands aggressively grabbing her crotch.

"*I want to fuck!*" she cried.

Julian stood in this boat, towering over the girl's body. The body was swaying from side to side with bigger and bigger movements, thrashing the small wooden boat against waves of water, bombarding the lake with a violent battering.

April lurched into the water and waded through. Once she reached the boat, she took a position at the end where Kaylee's head lay, holding it still. She clutched onto her with all her might, but still the boat swung from side to side, causing Julian to fall to his knees.

"Oscar, get over here!" she demanded, looking over her shoulder at him with a frantic glare.

Oscar jumped into the water, wading through, pushing against the resistance, willing himself quickly forward.

He reached the side of the boat by Kaylee's feet and held onto her ankles, gripping tightly until it hurt his fingers, doing all he could to steady it and give Julian the best chance.

Julian stood, balancing precariously, steadying himself with immense difficulty.

The demon was in hysterics. The little girl's mouth howled with echoing, deep, manic laughter. Its crotch rose slightly in the air, feet and arms stiffening like planks, convulsing in a seizure of malevolence.

Julian was not deterred. He withdrew his cross once more, kissing it, clutching it.

"Behold the cross of the Lord, the flee band of enemies," Julian spoke, even more assertively, removing the rosary beads from around his neck.

"The lion of the tribe of Juda," April spoke in response to Julian's words, tightening her grip on Kaylee's head until the veins of her hands stuck out. "The offspring of David hath conquered."

Julian held the cross out to the demon.

"I send you back to where you came from. Foul demon, you

may have taken us to steady water, but it is nothing like the pits of hell to which I will be sending you back, in God's almighty name."

For the first time, Oscar saw a flicker of terror across the demon's face.

"May thy mercy, Lord, descend upon us," Julian spoke, full of venomous confidence.

"As great as our hope in thee," April offered in response.

Julian dropped to his knees, Oscar quickly reacting to grip the boat hard and stop it from capsizing. Julian pressed the cross against Kaylee's heart and the demon cried out in pain, multiple anguished voices resounding from its mouth.

"From the snares of the devil!" Julian screamed out, clutching the cross harder and harder, pushing it further into the demon's face. The more he did this, the more the demon cried out in pain.

"Deliver us, oh Lord!" April answered, angry splashes drenching her chest.

"That thy church may serve thee in peace and liberty – free this girl!"

"Deliver us, oh Lord!"

The girl seized in an uncontrollable fit. A visible struggle entwined her face, dancing between a hateful, angry expression and innocent eyes of a young girl in torment. Oscar and April did all they could to hold the boat still, but it shook with such a mighty rage, swaying uncontrollably from side to side, thrashing water into Oscar's eyes.

"Crush down on all enemies of thy church, and release this girl in the name of God!"

"We beseech thee to hear us!"

The fit grew more and more violent until the girl was practically rising off the boat. April clambered into the wooden vessel, laying on top of her with all her weight to prevent Kaylee from flailing into drowning submission, meaning

Oscar had to put all his strength into holding the boat still by himself.

"I command you demon, in the name of God, to leave this body!"

"We beseech thee to hear us!"

April's eyes widened toward Oscar and she gestured with her eyebrows, encouraging him to join in the chant.

"Leave this girl, in the name of God!"

"We beseech thee to hear us!"

April waved her arm at Oscar to join in. He stood strong, full of assured resolve.

"In the name of God, I command you demon – *leave this girl!*"

Oscar joined in with April, "We beseech thee to hear us."

April mouthed at him, "Louder."

"I command you in the name of God, begone demon – be gone!"

"We beseech thee to hear us!" Oscar screamed out in unison with April.

The girl stiffened into a final contorted convulsion, then... nothing.

Her body lay flat on the boat.

Julian closed his eyes in satisfied exhaustion. April's panting grew still, calmly subsiding until she was knelt in a gently rocking boat, breathing every breath of anxiety out.

The boat's swaying back and forth lessened, tranquillity took over, until a loosely calm steady boat floated on a peaceful lake.

Oscar's mental state gradually changed; from feeling like he had a head full of stressed voices screaming and screaming at him, to a quiet, empty mind of passive equanimity.

"Is it done?" Oscar asked.

Julian gestured for Oscar to go to his side. Slowly, and with an affirmative glance at April who responded with an encouraging nod, Oscar meandered to Julian.

"You have the gift of being able to see these demons, Oscar," Julian told him. "I need you to place a hand on her head. I need you to tell me if it's gone."

"How will I know?"

"You will know if there is a demon there. Trust yourself."

Oscar stretched an arm over the girl, her eyes wide and terrified. They were no longer red, no longer fully dilated; but were two pained, hazy, mortified eyes, full of both relief and sadness.

Lowering his arm cautiously, he gently placed it on the girl's forehead. It was drenched with sweat, uncomfortably hot, and shivering manically. But he saw nothing.

There was no vision like before.

Nothing at all.

"It's gone," he confirmed.

Julian collapsed on the base of the boat beside a teary Kaylee. His shirt was drenched with lake water and perspiration, his face red, and his eyelids heavy.

April leant back, a hand resting on her forehead.

Her eyes turned to his.

She smiled. Nodded to him. And that was all he needed. He understood what it meant. "You did well, kid," or something along those lines.

It had worked.

The girl was safe.

The demon was gone.

Oscar looked down upon Kaylee's face once more. A solemn tear trickled down her cheek. She shook, a face wrapped up in relief and misery. Trauma that she still didn't fully understand.

"I want my mum..." she whispered.

Oscar nodded, and helped drag the boat to the side of the lake so they could take her back to her mother.

29

By the time Kaylee had limped and stumbled up the stairs, Nancy was on her knees.

Oscar struggled to remain unemotional as he stood in the doorway, watching mother and father reunited with their daughter.

Behind him, Julian still sat on the floor recovering. April was also resting after what had been a truly remarkably savage and enduring night, gently drying her hair with a kitchen towel.

But for Oscar, he couldn't avoid witnessing this moment.

Perhaps April and Julian were used to it. They were immune to the emotions involved, or they just learnt not to watch this moment occur to save themselves from emotional torment.

Oscar wanted to savour it.

Nancy clung to her daughter with tight, gripping arms wrapped in a desperate embrace. Her crying was loud, but she didn't care – and why should she? She had her daughter back.

Despite being in a cripplingly weakened state, Kaylee hugged tighter and tighter. None of the malevolent stares or sinister scowls remained. The sweet, innocent, extroverted child was back, though admittedly she was considerably wounded.

Oscar wasn't even sure what mental state she would be in. For anyone, enduring possession must be a hard, daunting experience; but for a girl so young, it must have been beyond traumatic.

As Oscar watched mother and daughter continue to cling to each other, to hug, to cry, to console each other's vastly externalised pain, his eyes drifted to Henry, the father.

Henry, who had also endured hard times. Being locked in a jail cell, accused of incredibly devastating allegations. He, too, must have a range of emotions.

Except, he didn't.

He stood still, expressionless. Watching his family reunite. His limp hand vaguely rubbed his wife's back in an attempt at frail reassurance. There was nothing about his face or body language that suggested he was flooded with complex feelings at the sight of this.

Still, people dealt with their emotions in different ways.

Maybe this was his way. Being stern and strong for his family.

Or maybe he was in fact guilty. Now it would come out.

Ridiculous thoughts. Stop it.

There was no doubt to be had.

This was a happy moment of a family sharing their love in their own ways, on what must be an overwhelming sense of relief.

Oscar felt a soft hand upon his back and recognised the touch as April's.

"Come on," she prompted him, walking forward and shaking Henry's hand.

"Thank you so much," Henry said, taking her hand firmly in his.

Maybe he was grateful then. Maybe he was just concealing his true state of mind.

Oscar looked over his shoulder to see if he could help tidy but found that Julian had somehow already packed everything up and was on his way.

Nancy stood and faced the Sensitives, still with her arms draped around her daughter.

"Please, stay," she insisted. "Let me do something for you. Make you tea, get you some wine, anything, I don't know…"

Julian planted a reassuring hand on her shoulder. "Please, you don't owe us anything. Enjoy having your family back. We have a long drive ahead of us."

"But I can't thank you enough…"

"Seeing you reunite with your daughter," Julian spoke sincerely, "is reward enough."

With a warm smile, a comforting nod, and a grateful handshake, he followed April down the stairs and through the front door.

Oscar nodded at Nancy, smiling as she continued to thank them. He then echoed Julian's sentiments in placing a reassuring hand on Henry's shoulder.

Then he paused.

There was something…

Henry smiled back at him.

And Oscar realised he was staying in the moment for too long. It was getting awkward.

So, with a nod, he followed his new companions out the front door and to the car.

"You can drive," Julian informed April, then turned to Oscar, "and you can ride up front. I'm laying down in the back and going to sleep. I am shattered."

"I'm not surprised," responded Oscar honestly.

By the time Oscar had found his seat in the front, watched

April turn the ignition, and looked over his shoulder at Julian – the guy was already asleep.

As April backed down the drive, Oscar watched the house grow smaller. He smiled resolutely as she directed the car to the motorway.

"How are you feeling?" April asked. "Your first exorcism. The first demon you've helped get rid of."

"I'm feeling… pretty good, April. Pretty good."

And for once, he was not lying.

He was feeling good.

He had helped do something worthwhile.

So he buried a deep, unsettling feeling that they were leaving something unfinished, and enjoyed the relaxing ride back down the M42 and onto the M5 toward his hometown of Tewkesbury.

30

The sign for junction 9 of the M5 passed by the window and the return journey was almost at an end.

Yet Oscar couldn't shake his bad feeling.

He glanced at the back seat where Julian was still asleep, then to April, who drove with a yawn. Neither of them seemed perturbed in the same way he was. They were the ones with the experience. The knowledge. Surely, if something wasn't entirely right, they would see it too.

Still, leaving the family's home just hadn't felt right.

It felt incomplete.

"What is it?" prompted April, noticing Oscar's discontent.

"Nothing," he lied. "I don't know. It's just…"

"Shocked?" April guessed. "First time, and you don't know how to react?"

"No, it's not that. I mean, it was shocking. But it's just…"

April signalled to turn off the motorway, taking the slip road toward the roundabout. Once she had slowed down and paused at the traffic lights, she turned an inquisitive stare to Oscar, trying to read him, uncomfortable at his unease.

"What?" she asked, more urgency in her voice. "What is it?"

"It just feels, I don't know, incomplete. Like there's something–"

Then it dawned on him.

A sudden flash.

As he left.

He nodded at Nancy. Smiling at her.

Then he turned to Henry.

Kaylee's father.

He placed a hand on his shoulder.

And then…

"Oh, God…" Oscar stuttered, lip trembling, arms shaking.

"What?" April frantically asked, trying to keep her eyes on the road at the same time as furiously glancing at Oscar. "What is it? What do you see?"

In Henry's eyes…

A flicker of fire faded to red. Henry's shadow engulfed the wall in a menacing shade of black, leering over the entire room, overwhelming their eyes with a black outline of shaded claws.

Behind Henry stood a beast.

Much like the one he had seen behind Kaylee at their first meeting, except this one was far bigger. Its carnivorous eyes and volcanic breath consumed the room in an air of fiery smoke. Oscar had an inexplicable feeling that he could not articulate – but was completely certain of – that he was in the presence of complete evil.

Oscar felt his body slip away. He began convulsing, seizing with large, fevered jolts. He foamed uncontrollably at the mouth, feeling the warm liquid soak his chin. In his vision, he saw a small black dot, a black dot that grew bigger and bigger, closer and closer, until that was all he saw.

Then he was back in the Kemple's house.

Standing before Henry Kemple.

With his reassuring hand on the father's shoulder, just where it had been before saying goodbye.

Except, there was something else. A beast. Guiding his every move with a dominant, snake-like arm, warped around Henry's throat like Henry was just a puppet, and this thing a puppeteer.

Behind this beastly figure were two grand wings ending in two points as sharp as a knife. Its tail spiralled from the rear end of its body, curling into a simmer of flames. Aside from a male torso, there was nothing human about it. Its face was ugly and treacherous, with a large nose, pointed fangs, and a head of hair Oscar first thought were dreadlocks, then realised were snakes. Its legs resembled that of a farm animal, with hairy, thick muscles ending in hooves that were home to three sharp curling, pointed claws.

This beast stood over Henry with a cocky grin, moving into its victim's body until its foul exterior had gone, soaking into every orifice and flake of skin of Henry.

Oscar's eyes shot open.

He lay on hard cement that dug into the back of his head. The car sat stationary beside him. April and Julian fussed over him, urging him to come to, repeatedly shouting his name.

As Oscar's vision refocussed, he rotated his head slightly, pulling a muscle in his neck. As he winced in pain, he realised he was on the hard shoulder of the slip road, laid on his back, his whole body aching from a violent fit.

"Relax, Oscar," Julian instructed, putting his arm out to halt April's frantic cries and replace them with his calming, soft voice. "It's okay."

Julian helped Oscar lean up, giving him a minute to take in where he was, to readjust, to come back down to earth.

"You scared us," Julian said.

Then Oscar remembered what he saw.

They didn't have much time.

His eyes opened wide with alarm, his hand clutching onto Julian's shoulders, his eyes shooting between him and April.

"We have to go back!" he cried out. "We have to go back!"

"Why, Oscar?" Julian asked, still keeping his cool. "What is it? What did you see?"

"It's Henry Kemple, her father…"

Julian's eyes grew wide with horror and his calm façade faded away as quickly as it had arrived.

"What about him?"

"The whole thing, the demon in Kaylee, she was just a pawn. Henry…"

"What about Henry?"

Oscar thought about Kaylee. A helpless little girl.

Nancy. A loving mother with no idea what danger she and her daughter were in.

Then Henry.

"Oh, God…"

HENRY SAT BACK IN HIS ARMCHAIR, ALLOWING THE BODY TO rest.

It was an older body than Lilu was used to.

But it was the only choice available.

Lilith had done her task, but unfortunately, she was done. Removed. Failed.

Pathetic, weak little girl.

The woman he loved more than hell itself, but still a disappointment.

Lilu would not be so easy to fight.

Nancy had made Kaylee some tea. Beans on toast. As Kaylee devoured it, Nancy dabbed at her wounds with a wet flannel. A whole medical kit spread out across the living room floor.

Ridiculous human.

She thinks a few little cuts on a face are going to hurt?

She thinks nursing her daughter with love and rainbows and happiness will save her from what was to come?

He grew sick of her. How much longer did he have to endure of this pitiful imbecile?

Kaylee flinched from the pressure on her wound.

"Oh, my baby, I'm so sorry," Nancy spoke.

So weak. So eager to protect.

He stood.

Contemplated.

Watched.

"Where are you going?" Nancy asked, not moving her loving gaze from her wounded daughter.

He ignored her, stepping heavily and precisely out of the room, into the kitchen. He opened drawers, looked in cupboards, searched the sink.

Finally, he grew tired of looking. There was a solid, robust, toaster on the side.

That would do.

He ripped the toaster from the wall, took it into the living room, and stood over Nancy.

Nancy peered up at him from her kneeling position beside her daughter, eyes full of confusion.

"What are you doing with the toaster?" she asked innocently.

He held it above his head.

"Henry?"

With all the force that this body had, with all the muscles available, he brought the toaster soaring downwards and thrust it into her forehead with lethal force.

Kaylee jumped, her beans on toast flinging off her lap, cowering against the wall.

Nancy crawled along the floor. Dizzy. Shocked.

She dabbed her forehead and looked up.

"What are you doing?" she feebly uttered.

Her entire face was covered in trickling blood, accompanied by a beautifully grey bruise.

Lovely.

He lunged the toaster back down, sinking it into her head with excessive force and relative ease.

"Henry!" she wept, struggling to her knees.

He struck her with the toaster again.

This time she didn't move.

He brought it back down and slammed it into her head. Again. Again and again.

And again.

And again.

And again.

He threw the toaster to the side, discarding it like a finished chocolate wrapper. He took hold of a clump of her hair in his sweaty fist and lifted her head up.

Her eyes hazed over with a groggy absence. She gurgled an oozing of blood that went trickling down her chin. Her nose bent to the side, teeth fell past her cracked lip, and most of her pale skin was covered in dark-grey bruising.

He dragged her across the room by the hair, reaching a wooden television stand.

He launched her head into the television, sending her cranium flying into a cracked, sparking mess. Keeping hold of her hair, he lifted her head once more and drove her skull down into the solidity of the wooden surface.

He kept going until her face was elegantly unrecognisable.

He threw her on the floor.

She did not move.

He climbed on top of her and slid his hands around her neck, tightening his grip.

But he didn't need to.

He already felt no pulse.

He dropped her body to the floor like a discarded piece of waste.

With a triumphant smirk, he slowly turned his head to the other side of the room.

Kaylee cowered in the corner. Too scared to move. Her eyes wide in terror.

It was just the two of them.

Alone at last.

OSCAR GAGGED OVER THE BUSHES, SPEWING A STRINGY BUT thick mouthful of gunk. This vision was not any more tolerable than the last.

But he needed to get over it.

There was more on the line than his weak stomach.

He limped down the garden path and into the home of April and Julian. Being only minutes from the motorway, they had rushed Oscar into the back seat and sped back as fast as they could.

As he returned to the house, Julian's frantic voice hit Oscar like a bombardment on his ear-drums. He made his way to the kitchen, where April sat at the table. She had dissolved some disprin into a small glass of water that she passed to Oscar, and he gratefully drank.

Julian burst into the kitchen, slamming his mobile phone down on the table.

"There's no answer," he declared, turning around, nervously fidgeting. He paced back and forth, covering every tile of the kitchen floor.

"Shouldn't we go back?" Oscar asked, trying to look away

from Julian, as the pacing was making his fuzzy head even dizzier.

Julian ignored him, stuck between various thoughts, none of which seemed to be offering a solution.

"It's a two-hour drive," April replied, placing a comforting hand on Oscar's. "We won't get there in time."

"Surely we need to try? I mean, we can't just sit here and do nothing."

Julian pulled a laptop out of the drawer and slammed it on the table, hurriedly loading it.

"We will," he assured Oscar. "But we need to get in contact with Nancy first and tell her to get her and Kaylee out of the house. I'm going to have to go online, see if there's any other number or way of contacting her."

"I don't get it," Oscar said, a face full of torturous guilt. "How come I'm only getting this vision now, when I touched his shoulder before we left?"

Julian was too absorbed in his futile attempts at finding more contact information, so April took it upon herself to answer.

"Sometimes really powerful demons can block glimpses about themselves," April took over. "It could be that the block dropped once you got far enough away, or that the demon stopped."

"What I still don't get," Julian venomously announced as he clicked harshly on the mouse, "is who the fuck this demon is."

Oscar let a moment pass before answering. He was new, and didn't want to upset anyone – but he was fairly sure he had the answer.

"Didn't you say Kaylee's demon was part of a pair?"

Julian looked up, irritated. "Yes."

"Maybe the girl was possessed by the lower demon. And Henry was taken by the one in charge, and now we are dealing with something all the more powerful, who has been leading the whole thing all along."

Julian and April shared an embarrassed glance.

"I mean," Oscar continued, "that would explain why the girl dropped the accusation, and the dad went free. That could have been when... you know..."

Oscar's voice faded, feeling a little disconcerted by the humiliated look the other two were sharing. Had he over-stepped?

"That was..." April began, looking once more at Julian. "... brilliant, Oscar. I don't know why we didn't think of that..."

She looked to Julian once more, who nodded vaguely, the only admittance Oscar knew he would get from him.

April nodded at him, at first shocked at his progression, then with a playful smile that revealed a new admiration.

In a new sudden burst of anger, Julian slammed the lid.

"Nothing," he declared. "Let's just pray there is no late-night traffic to stand in our way."

3 3

Henry's coarse foot kicked Nancy's head further into the cupboard beneath the stairs. A cluttered assortment of useless crap fell on her, remnants of pointless possessions hidden away and never used.

Soon it would all be divided up in a will or thrown into a skip.

Nancy's head would not get inside, so in the end, he resorted to having to lift the corpse by the hair, and push it inside with his foot and shut the door quickly before her dead weight fell back upon it.

She was heavier than she looked.

How could Henry have ever fucked that? She was so... human.

He glanced at the time. The police needed to hurry up. It had been at least half an hour since he had called.

He didn't have much time.

The blocking would have worn off. That scrawny little rag-boy would have had a vision by now. Some kind of glimpse that showed the truth about who was inside Henry's body.

Why did the little shit have to touch him on the shoulder?

The kid was almost gone. Leaving. The deed had been done. He was going to be left to it, nothing to stop what he was about to do with this family.

Then the fucking prick touched his shoulder.

A loud, authoritative knock resounded three times against the front door.

Right.

Time to be Henry the father.

I'm upset.

He forced tears out of this mortal, weak body. He bounced on the spot, getting red to his cheeks, forcing himself to be out of breath.

Fucking humans.

He flung open the door.

"Oh, thank God you're here!" he declared through Henry's subordinate mouth, ushering the police officer in.

"My name is Detective Inspector Jason Lyle," the man told him, showing a badge. "I was at your daughter's interrogation."

"Yes, yes, I remember you!" Henry declared, weeping eyes and distraught frown displaying a manner of distress that clearly irritated Jason.

Good.

That would mean it was convincing.

"You told me someone abused your daughter," Jason prompted.

"Yes, yes I did. They came here claiming they were going to help her do all this voodoo stuff. We thought they were good people. At first…"

Henry's hand quickly withdrew his phone and held it out to Jason, a video ready to play.

Lilu watched, surveying the reaction of the officer. He didn't need to see the video to know what images accompanied the vile sounds. So, instead, he studied the detective's reactions. Making sure the shocking images recorded were having their effect.

He watched as Jason Lyle viewed the video of Julian performing an exorcism on Kaylee.

A video that, out of context, looked very bad.

A girl being pinned down on a bed, where she lay in restraints. Jason flinging holy water on her, crosses pressed against her, doing nothing to avert the agonising screams of the poor little girl.

"Once I saw what they were doing," he whimpered, "I tried to stop them. But they just wouldn't. They said they had to make her pure again, then they just kept saying it over and over."

The video ended, and Jason lifted his perturbed visage to Henry.

"And this happened tonight?" Jason asked.

"Yes, it did."

"Have you got a name for this man?"

"Yes. His name is Julian Barth. He claims to be part of some paranormal investigation team from Gloucestershire, calling themselves Sensitives, or something."

"That's the people your lawyers called, was it not?"

"Yes, yes it was, and that was why we trusted them! Oh, we trusted them!"

He considered for a moment whether the last "oh, we trusted them" was too much, but Jason seemed to buy it.

"I'm going to need you and your family to come down to the station and give a statement."

"Kaylee has just gone to sleep; can it wait until the morning?"

"Not really. If we are to arrest this man, we are going to need to take a statement as quickly as we can – time is important, you see."

"I know, but it's been such an ordeal. We'll wake her up in an hour, please, just give us that."

Jason peered peculiarly at Henry.

"In an hour, then, I really must insist."

"We will be there."

"In the meantime, I will contact Gloucestershire about this man. I will need to take this phone, Mr. Kemple."

"Oh, please do."

A creak echoed in the hallway.

Jason peered past Henry at the door to the cupboard under the stairs that had opened very slightly.

"Is everything else okay, Mr. Kemple?" he asked.

"Oh yes, fine, yes."

"I will see you in an hour then."

With another glance down the corridor, Jason turned and walked away, closing the door behind him.

He watched through the window as the police car drove away.

Then he turned. Walked upstairs. Into the little girl's room.

There, Kaylee sat helplessly bound to a chair, duct tape wrapped multiple times around her mouth and body. Her wide, terrified eyes peered up at the face of her loving father, so vastly changed from the man she knew.

"You let them take my Lilith from me," he declared

He bent over, placing his hands on his knees in a way that was so patronising it became mortifyingly sadistic.

"She was what they call a succubus. Do you remember?"

Her eyes flinched.

"I'm not sure if you do. Do you know what succubus means?"

He placed a gentle hand on the side of her face.

A pleasurably sordid grin spread wide across his face, pushing his cheeks into an unsettling leer.

"How about I show you?"

THE HOUSE BUSTLED WITH HASTE. JULIAN'S EXORCISM essentials were restocked and flung back into his leather-bound bag. April clutched the car keys tight and had her trainers back on before Oscar even acknowledged they were moving.

Oscar tried to keep up. Tried to maintain the urgency set by the other two.

A family's lives were at stake.

A mother. A daughter. Both who could already be dead.

As April nodded in confirmation that she was ready and Julian turned his expectant stare to Oscar – the doorbell rang.

They looked at each other, confused.

Julian opened the door and cast his eyes upon two tall, muscular police officers.

"Julian Barth?" one of them prompted in a thick country accent.

"Yes…" he answered, glancing back at April, a look of hesitant terror on his face. "Can I help you?"

"We are going to need you to come with us."

"Is this really necessary? As we have somewhere to be quite urgently."

The two police officers shot each other a look as if they were confirming something, making a silent decision.

"Julian Barth, you are under arrest on suspicion of causing significant harm to an underage child under the Children Act 1989," one of them stated matter-of-factly.

"For *what?*"

"You do not have to say anything, but it may harm your defence if you do not mention when questioned something which you later rely on in court. Anything you do say may be given in evidence."

The officer went to take hold of Julian's arm, but he flinched it away.

"Listen, lad," the officer began, "it's up to you whether you come with us willingly, or whether you come in the handcuffs."

Julian froze, the conundrum of his perilous decision of whether to submit or defy these officers presented clearly upon his face.

But what was he going to do?

He had no way out of this. No way to get to the Kemples without the police interfering and halting the whole process.

He turned to April and whispered a sudden thought of stark realisation.

"It's the dad," he gasped. "He knows we know."

"Come on, son," the policeman demanded, grabbing hold of Julian's arm and dragging him out.

April and Oscar stood helplessly watching, faces like a child saying goodbye to their parents on the first day of school.

"What are we going to do?" Oscar asked April.

April had no answer.

She simply bowed her head and shook it.

"What can we do? He's the exorcist. He's the one who knows how to do this stuff."

"But we can't just let—"

"We can't do anything about it!" she snapped.

After she watched the police car disappear down the street and turn the corner, she shut the door with a ferocious, agitated slam.

Oscar searched for an answer, but he didn't have one.

"They are on their own," April declared.

THIS IS WHAT YOU GET WHEN YOU TRY TO DO SOMETHING GREAT in a world that people don't understand.

You get burnt at the stake for it.

And it's infuriating.

And April was so, so fed up.

Just because the world hadn't seen what they'd seen. Because the world wasn't open-minded enough to believe what they must. Because the world was infantile and cruel and pathetic and–

"Fuck," April muttered within a sickened sigh.

She sat on the stairs, her head rested against the wall, vacantly watching the door that Julian had departed through not too long ago.

These ignorant people had no idea what they were doing.

But what was she meant to do without Julian?

Julian was the one who'd taken her off the streets. Given her a home. Shown her what to do. Led her.

Without his skill set, she was useless.

She was a conduit and a glimpser – not an exorcist.

"Hey," came Oscar's soft voice.

April moved only her eyes, choosing to remain slumped miserably against the wall. She looked at Oscar edging into view, leaning against the wall of the hallway.

Now really wasn't the time.

She didn't have the patience for his inexperience and ridiculously low self-esteem.

She wished he would go away.

"How you doing?" he asked, a face full of concern.

"How do you think I'm doing?" she snapped.

She knew she should be nicer to him. He was trying to make sure she was okay. But she didn't care.

She wanted to be alone.

"There was nothing you could have done," he reassured her.

"Piss off, Oscar," April instructed. "Not in the mood."

Oscar's head dropped. His hands went into his pockets and his whole body slouched into a hunched posture, curling over into his easily intimidated, withdrawn stance.

He retracted back into the other room.

He looked downbeat and downtrodden, but April didn't care.

April didn't care about anything.

An innocent family was likely about to die.

Without Julian, she was nothing. She couldn't attempt an exorcism. God knows Oscar couldn't.

It was useless.

April jumped as a bag was thrown to the ground before her. Scowling irritably at the leather-bound bag that contained all of Julian's items, she turned her anger to Oscar who had re-entered the hallway, and now stood over it.

"What are you doing?" April demanded through clenched teeth and stiffened jaw.

"I'm going to Loughborough," he announced. "Are you coming with me?"

April shook her head.

Pathetic.

"You're not going to Loughborough," she replied.

"Oh yes, I am!" Oscar declared, grinning wildly. "I'm going to go do everything I can to save that family."

"We are nothing without Julian, don't be ridiculous."

"Yes," Oscar confirmed, nodding as he took a moment to think about his choice of words. "But I'm still going to try."

"Oscar, as lovely as this whole thing is, we wouldn't survive it. Without Julian there to help–"

"Yeah, well, Julian isn't there to help, is he?"

April tilted her head back and sighed.

"So we're going to have to do it without him," Oscar decided.

"Get a grip man, you can't do this–"

"Can't do this?" Oscar repeated, waving his arms in astonishment. "Five days ago, I thought I couldn't survive without my medication. Five days ago, I thought ghosts or demons didn't exist, never mind that I could fight them. And five days ago, I thought no woman would ever talk to me."

April looked away, blushing.

"And then you came along," Oscar continued, crouching before April, beseeching her with his eyes. "And you showed me that I can do those things."

"Oscar–"

"And now it's time for me to show you what you can do."

Her eyes met his and she felt truly warm inside. Yes, he was young, and stupid, and scruffy, and immensely irritating. But he had kind eyes, a warm smile, and the best of intentions.

"So I'm going, with or without you. But I'd rather it was with you. So what do you say, April? Are you coming?"

Beneath the ridiculous boyish exterior, he was a sweet man. And he made her feel like she could do anything.

And she could do anything.

"Yes," she answered. "But I'm driving."

OSCAR'S HANDS GRIPPED THE SIDES OF THE PASSENGER SEAT, flinching his eyes away from the sight before him. He had never been in a car going so fast. Every car in the other lanes of the M5 were just blurs.

Oscar glanced at the speedometer beside the steering wheel that April was clutching with eager alarm.

I didn't even know a car could go that fast...

"So how long since you passed your test?" Oscar inquired, trying to find something that could reassure his dangerously high blood pressure.

"I'm taking it next week."

"What?"

Oscar decided the best thing to do would be to close his eyes really tightly and pretend he was somewhere else.

But he couldn't do that.

Because every time he closed his eyes, he saw it again.

The father. The demon. Standing over him.

Then, just as April recklessly merged the car across three lanes and onto the M42, the visions hit him once more.

They took his breath away like he'd been sucker punched.

He gasped for breath as he fought the invasive thoughts that just kept coming and coming.

The horns. The serpentine snake-ish legs. The cackling grimace of the mouldy, cracked lips upon its ugly face.

Then he came to. Sweating and panting, he could once more see the road before him.

"Hold on, Oscar," April urged him. "Come on, stay with me."

He turned toward her, but before he could register the concern on her face, he was gone again.

This time he was looking up at Henry.

Henry was bringing a toaster.

Why was he bringing a toaster?

He looked to his side. Kaylee sat beneath him, devouring a plate of baked beans on toast.

Then he realised.

I'm Nancy. This is what Nancy saw.

He fell to the floor with a sudden blow, his entire body jolting.

His eyes flung open and he was back in the car, but he was seizing, his body uncontrollably convulsing.

"I need my medication!" Oscar screamed. "Only my medication can stop this!"

"No!" April defied. "You cannot have it. You have to do this yourself."

"But I can't!" Oscar wailed, his arms helplessly reaching out.

He slipped back again.

He was looking up. In a living room. Henry was above him.

Blood was trickling into his eyes. He could feel it oozing, dripping in a gulp of thick mess.

But he didn't have time to wipe it.

Henry brought the toaster down onto his head once more.

His eyes jerked open.

April was frantically switching her gaze between the road and Oscar. Looking back and forth, back and forth.

"Nancy..." Oscar whimpered. "She's dead... He's killed her..."

"What?"

"I saw it... He's killed her..."

"What about Kaylee? Is Kaylee okay?"

He was back in the living room, being dragged by a large mound of hair toward a television.

Kaylee was at the end of the room, cowering in a ball. Crying. Weeping. Desperately abandoned.

His head went into the television.

A smash and a set of sparks fluttered over his vision.

"My medication, please..."

"No, Oscar, control it!"

His head smashed into the wooden table.

Everything went dark. Hazy.

Nothing but the sound of a skull being bludgeoned into wood.

Then it occurred to him.

If I die in a vision – do I die in real life?

"I'm about to die..." Oscar cried out.

"Stop it! Get a grip!"

The smell of freshly polished wood.

The sound of bones cracking into pieces.

The taste of thick blood trickling down his throat, choking him, coughing on loose teeth.

"Oscar – you are in control. You are the master of these glimpses."

His eyes opened briefly.

April's worried face looked down upon him.

He was in a heap on the floor of the car.

"Come on, Oscar."

The pain of a smashed cranium consumed him. His nervous system shattered.

"Oscar – I believe you can do this."

April.

April believes.

April believes I can do this.

His fists turned to a tight grip. Clenching for war. Readying his body for the fight.

Everything was no longer blank.

He stood up.

He left Nancy's body, backed away.

Watching as Henry continued to pummel her head into the wooden surface.

Watched as Kaylee continued to cower in the corner.

April.

April believes.

April knows I can do this. She's said it all along.

No more.

I am in control.

Oscar closed his eyes, scrunching his face, screaming so hard it felt like razor blades dragging through his throat.

Enough.

Enough being a loser.

Enough medication.

Enough being some going-nowhere, jacking off, pathetic little piece of shit.

A boy backs down and lets these things control him.

April.

A man stands up and takes control.

April believes.

Thank you, April.

His eyes flung open.

Manically sweating, blood rushing to his head.

He sat up. Looked around himself.

He was in a car, going one hundred miles per hour.

His panting subsided.

He wiped the sweat from his brow.

He turned to April.

"Thank you," he spoke.

April smiled, then turned her attention to driving.

Finally, he was in control.

JASON STOOD SOLEMNLY OUTSIDE THE POLICE STATION, SOAKING up the peaceful night sky. The stars were shining brightly. There was a slight breeze lingering in the air, and there was minimal activity around the station. It was rare to have such a quiet night, and he wasn't sure whether he liked it. As an officer, you live for the busy nights but pray for the quiet ones.

He checked his watch.

It had been two hours.

Henry Kemple should have brought his family to the station by now.

A police car turned into the station car park and interrupted his trail of thought. He recognised instantly the face in the back as being the one from the video and gazed at him with morose curiosity.

Wanting to make sure this guy knew who was the boss, he stood tall, stiffening his posture, ensuring his feet were shoulder-width apart and his arms were sturdily folded.

The driver's window wound down and the officer turned to Jason.

"You Detective Inspector Jason Lyle?"

"I am," Jason nodded. "This my suspect?"

"Yeah. Where do you want him?" the officer asked as if he was delivering a parcel.

"Bring him out, I'll take him in."

The two officers stood out from the car, opened the back door, and brought the suspect out.

Julian Barth was a tidy man, mid-20s, completely unsuspicious.

But then again, they all are, aren't they?

No one can truly predict an abuser by looking at them.

"Thank you." Jason directed the officers as he took hold of Julian by the arm. "Much appreciated."

Jason led Julian into the station and booked him in. All the time, watching him. Studying him. He liked to do this with all his suspects, and had done so for fifteen years. Making sure he knew what to expect. If they were heavy, could they use their weight against him? If they were short, could they be nimble?

But as he directed Julian through to the cells, he saw nothing from him that would indicate a threat. If anything, the man seemed to be seething under his breath the entire time, as if muttering in angst.

Then, just as he was about to shut the door, Julian spoke.

"Do you have any idea what you're doing?"

Jason paused. He didn't normally waste time listening to the angry ramblings of perpetrators once he had locked them in the cell.

But it was something about this case.

About the girl.

Something had unsettled him...

He remained blank, strong in his body language, hovering in the doorway. Julian now sat on the bed, his head in his hands, his legs bouncing agitatedly.

"That girl is in serious danger," Julian claimed.

"Not anymore," Jason spoke, softly yet assertively.

"Her father is not what you think he is."

Jason folded his arms and leant against the side of the doorway, lifting an eyebrow.

"From what I've seen of the cruelty you've committed–"

"I gave her an exorcism!" Julian shouted, immediately giving Jason the balance of control. "I don't have time to sit here and argue with you about whether or not ghosts and demons exist, but they do – and they were in her. And now they are in her dad. And he is going to *kill* her if I don't do anything."

"See, what gets me – is I can't figure out whether you've made this all up, or whether you actually believe it yourself."

"For God's sake, you don't understand!"

Julian stood as if to lurch himself forward and plead. Jason abruptly held his arm out and went to shut the door, as if preparing for an attack, prompting Julian to instantly put his hands in the air and stand back.

"I'm not going to attack you," Julian promised.

"Damn right you're not."

"I just need you to understand."

Jason nodded patronisingly.

"I think I understand all right."

Jason went to shut the door.

"Wait!"

Jason didn't speak, but hovered the door slightly ajar, so he could just see Julian within the crack.

"You've worked this case, right?"

Jason didn't answer.

"I'm taking that as a yes. So, I'm assuming you spoke to this girl when she was arrested. That you interrogated her, and her dad."

Jason raised his eyebrows.

"Well, did you not think there was something off about

her? Was she acting in the way you would expect a sweet little middle-class girl to do?"

Jason considered this.

She wasn't.

But that meant nothing.

"Was she?" Julian repeated, his hands stretched out in desperation. He looked like he thought he was getting somewhere.

True, this girl was strange.

But at no point did that mean demons suddenly existed.

As Jason backed away, he just about heard Julian shout one more thing.

"Play it backwards! Play it–"

Jason closed the door and locked the cell.

THE PEACEFUL NIGHT CAST A TRANSLUCENT GLOW OVER THE tranquil evening.

Oscar and April didn't give a shit.

As April haphazardly swung the car onto the Kemple's drive, an overwhelming sense of dread filled Oscar like a bucket of poison filtering through his body.

It was one thing to persuade April they should drive up to Loughborough and fight this thing. It was another thing entirely to step out of the car and face an evil entity from hell that could very well kill you.

Glimpses filled Oscar's head, and he was finally starting to get a loose grip over these crushing visions. So long as he retained his calm head and kept his breathing slow, he was in control.

As he stepped out of the car and stood beside April, the house flashed red. A splatter of blood appeared on the inside of the living room window, vanishing as quickly as it appeared.

An omen of what may have already happened, or so Oscar assumed.

"I don't like this," April admitted.

"You kidding?" Oscar scoffed, turning to her. "You're the one I'm relying on."

"It's just too quiet."

She was right.

An eerie stillness lingered around the house. A silence that screamed too loudly. There were no lights, no flickers of shadows, no sign of life whatsoever. Just a feeling of destitution, as if something bad had either happened or was about to happen. Or both.

April began the cautious steps forward, prompting Oscar to follow. His legs wobbled, buckling weakly under the anxiety that filled his gut.

Everything about this was wrong.

Everything about this told Oscar to back away.

But he couldn't. He had come this far.

"Should we knock?" Oscar asked April, realising he hadn't thought this far ahead.

April shook her head.

He tried opening the door, but it opened about an inch until it stopped suddenly.

"I think it's on a latch," Oscar decided.

"Well, you're a strong man."

Oscar frowned at the ridiculous assertion. Just an excuse for him to do his shoulder in, rather than her.

Still, it made him gush, and he couldn't let her down.

He took a step back and barged against the door. It buckled slightly but did not falter. So he leant back and barged against it once more, forcing the door to swing back against the inside wall.

Oscar glanced at April, feeling smug, to see if she was impressed. Her eyes remained focussed as she stepped inside, Oscar following and shutting the door behind them.

It was pitch-black, except for the clock on the oven in the

far kitchen and the moonlight through the windows of the nearby living room.

It took a few moments for Oscar's eyes to adjust. He scanned the vacant rooms. The stairs to his right, the living room to his left, the kitchen ahead of him.

There were too many places for something to jump out.

Too many places for them to get caught.

"Where to?" Oscar whispered to April.

"We need to find Nancy and Kaylee, get them out," April urged.

Taking a wary step forward, Oscar jumped at the sound of a creak. Not looking behind him to avoid the humiliation of seeing April's face at his immense fear, he looked for the source of the creak.

The downstairs cupboard, beneath the stairs.

The door was slightly open, something resting upon it from the inside, forcing it to buckle marginally beneath the pressure.

Oscar looked at April, who nodded toward it, urging him to open it.

Summoning all the courage he could, he placed his sweaty palm on the handle and swung it open.

The dead body of Nancy fell to their feet, her bludgeoned head covered in dried blood. One of her eyes could be made out beneath the smashed skull, staring rigidly up at Oscar.

For the second night running, Jason sat in his office, his mind dwelling on the chilling case of Kaylee Kemple.

For the second night running, a half-empty cup sat on his desk, home to cold coffee and broken biscuit. The night birds hooted and tweeted outside the open window of his stuffy office, accompanying his deep contemplation with a gentle background noise to a station that was otherwise silent.

Something Julian Barth had said to him was severely troubling.

"Did you not think there was something off about her?"

Well, honestly, yes. Jason did. But that didn't mean holding a girl down and disguising child abuse with aged religious concepts was a valid excuse.

He picked up his phone and dialled the Kemple's number.

"Hello, you have reached Henry Kemple. I'm not able to get to the phone right now, so please leave a message at the beep."

Irritated, Jason clutched the phone with exasperation.

"Yes, hello, this is Detective Inspector Jason Lyle. Mr. Kemple, you were meant to come down the station an hour after we spoke. This was over two hours ago now. Please, can you let me know what is taking so long? If you don't come down, this may mean we will have to let the suspect go without charge. Get back to me."

He hung up, slamming the phone on the desk.

It was strange. Really, really strange.

That Henry Kemple called Jason to his house to show him this video, prompting him to arrest Julian, then does not show to give his statement.

Why would he do that?

Julian kept insinuating there was something Jason did not know about.

So what was it?

Once again, he opened his laptop and loaded the CCTV video of the interrogation with Kaylee.

Again, she sat there, so still. Her body so perfectly symmetrical, all her joints entwined within a rigid position. Her legs beneath her arms that lay neatly on the table. So innocently deprived. So haphazardly sweet and evil.

"My daddy molested me," she announced in a sickening voice that seemed so... fakely sweet.

What was she doing?

Then it happened.

A brief flicker, where it looked like a cloud appeared on the screen. In less than a second, it was gone.

What was that?

Why hadn't he seen it before?

Jason stopped the video and dragged the bar back to the beginning, playing it once more.

"My daddy molested me."

Sure enough, it happened again. So quickly it would be missed in a blink. Half a second looking away, one would never realise it was there.

He scrolled the video back once more, but this time went

frame by frame. Clicking the mouse then waiting, seeing if it showed up.

Nothing.

Then...

Jason practically fell off his chair. He clambered backwards, backing away from the screen in horror.

He stood.

Paced back and forth a few times.

Opened out the window. Had some fresh air. Drank the rest of his cold coffee.

"What the fuck..."

Then, once he was mentally ready, he turned back to the screen once more.

There, behind the girl, was a form of smoke, appearing for a single frame. But it wasn't just any smoke; it was in the shape of a figure, with horns, a baby, the tail of a snake.

It was just a cloud of smoke.

A cloud of smoke taking the elusive shape of... What? A ghost? A demon?

He was seeing things.

It was nothing.

A blip on the recording. A coincidence.

Then he recalled the last thing Julian had said as he shut the cell door.

"Play it backwards!"

Play it backwards... Could he have meant the interview?

He hit the reverse button.

And there, in clear, audible words, he heard it. The words that had said "my daddy molested me" in a detestable, freakish voice, now said something different:

"Please help me."

No. It can't be. I'm going crazy.

Maybe he should show this to someone?

"Please help me. Please help me," it repeated again and again and again.

He hit stop.

He had to show this to someone. He had to.

No. They would think I am crazy. This is ridiculous.

He thought about playing it again but didn't need to.

In a fit of dizziness, he stumbled out the door, knocking a stack of papers off his desk as he did. He barged through the empty corridors to the cell block, marching toward Julian's cell.

He banged on the cell door to get Julian's attention. Julian stood up from his bed, approaching Jason, who leered haphazardly through the window.

"What is going on?" Jason cried out.

"That girl was possessed, and we freed her. Now the father is possessed, and is likely going to kill her as a result."

Jason backed away.

What was going on?

Was he really doing this?

Oh, God...

"Can she still be saved?" Jason urgently demanded. "If I get us there with blue lights, can she still be saved?"

Julian shrugged. "She may well already be dead, but it's worth a shot."

Jason nodded and tripped on his way to get the keys, trying to keep himself steady, in disbelief at what he was doing.

4 0

IT TOOK EVERYTHING OSCAR HAD TO FIGHT HIS GAG REFLEX.

It was the first time he had ever seen a dead body, and the emasculated part of him wished he could say he handled it better. Something he may have been able to do if the body hadn't been such a deformed, mangled, distorted corpse.

"Pull yourself together," April urged him.

He nodded vacantly, unaware he was even responding. His eyes remained transfixed on the lifeless eyes staring vacantly back at him.

April nudged him and pulled his face toward hers.

"I need you, Oscar. Don't flake out on me now."

She needs me?

Not caring that he was probably taking that the completely opposite way to which it was intended, he decided she was right. He was acting how the old Oscar would have acted.

No more.

This was the new Oscar.

A clang of heavily falling furniture thudded against the ceiling above, vibrating a cloud of dust off the wooden beams.

Oscar and April exchanged a silent glance of confirmation. They were heading upstairs.

Reaching into the bag April had brought in, Oscar withdrew a cross and clutched onto it.

So silly, really. A week ago he refused to even set foot in a church, what with how ridiculous a concept religion was.

Now here he was, clutching onto a cross in the hope it was going to keep him alive.

Step by step, he crept. Placing one gentle foot above the other, placing them down with enough care so as to avoid the creak of the old wooden floorboards beneath the faded carpet.

As he approached the landing, he peered across the dark hallway. The girl's room, at the far end of the corridor, gifted them a tiny crack, with a minuscule shaft of light shining out.

Oscar hesitated.

Exhaled deeply.

April took hold of his hand and grasped it, squeezing it tightly in comfort.

Oscar appreciated it.

It wasn't just about how being able to hold her hand filled his body with excited tingles, but the reassurance it gave him to feel her soft skin against his.

It gave him the strength to take the final few steps.

With a deep breath he gathered himself, filling his mind with calm thoughts to quell the rabid anxiety coursing through him.

He lunged himself forward and barged through the door, holding his cross out, gripping it so tightly the edges splintered painfully into his palm.

Fuck the pain.

It was time to step up.

It took a moment of repulsion for him to ignore the sight before him. Willing it to fade into the background, he urged himself to overcome it.

The girl was laid in a bloody heap upon the bed. Oscar could see her chest rising up and down, slowly taking in what air she could – a sign that she was still alive, at least. But her face was badly bruised, her body cut, her clothes ripped and torn.

Henry turned his head toward Oscar and April with a devious growl. It was inhuman – like an alerted wild animal turning toward its prey. From the position Henry held over Kaylee, Oscar dreaded to think about what the poor girl's father was doing.

The guy was almost unrecognisable.

What had been neatly groomed, gelled hair was now a sweaty mess mixed with patches of blood. His eyes were large circles of red. His skin was barely present, faded to a dark-pale scar, wrinkled with wounds. His mouth was black, with blood seeping through the cracks of his teeth, and his torn lips lifted uncomfortably at a skewed angle across his face. White blotches of scar tissue decorated his eyelids.

But what freaked Oscar out most was Henry's body. Every joint was distorted, bent in a way that was unnatural for a human's bones to bend, turning in every direction he shouldn't.

His growl was merciless. A mixture of various carnivorous animals, a scream that sent Oscar against the back of the wall.

But Oscar was not letting this thing win.

The poor girl looked to have been tortured to the edge of her life, and it was up to him to provide her salvation.

"Back away, you foul beast!" Oscar demanded, holding his cross out.

April joined him, clutching rosary beads toward the demonic creature before them.

Oscar did his best to remember the prayer Julian had used.

"In the name of the Father, the Son, and the Holy Spirit, leave this being!"

A sinister smirk grew across Henry's crooked face.

"The angels in heaven command you!"

The angels in heaven? That wasn't it, was it?

The grin turned into a malevolent chuckle.

"The power of Christ demands you to let this man go!"

In an effortless swipe, Henry's claw swung over the cross and rosary beads, knocking them to the floor.

It stood, facing them.

Oscar cowered. Glanced at April. Lip quivering.

Was this it?

Was this how he was about to die?

The first time he ever tried doing the right thing in his entire life was going to be the last thing he ever did?

That was when, in a huge stroke of good fortune, the door swung open.

In stormed a police officer named Jason Lyle, followed by the strong march of Julian, holding his own cross, demanding the demon away.

JASON DOVE ON HENRY, TAKING HIM TO THE GROUND, PINNING him down with all of his weight.

Jason's jaw dropped at the sight of Henry's face. It was an animalistic mess – its glare intensified like a rabid beast, snarling and snapping its jaw at Jason, excessive saliva dripping down his chin in bloody gunks.

Julian held his cross toward Henry.

"Dear heavenly Father," Julian began.

But it wasn't enough.

Henry soared into the air and, before Jason could understand what was happening, he had been smacked into the ceiling. He cried with pain as he was held there for a moment, the bump of the lamp digging into his back as it gave off sparks that sent violent shivers up and down his body. Henry then plummeted back to the floor, shaking like a dog drying itself so as to knock Jason away from him.

Jason's groaning body rolled onto the floor.

Everything hurt. Every bone, every muscle.

He lifted his head slowly, dragging his hazy vision upwards. He saw what was on the bed.

Kaylee.

Tied to the bed by each wrist and ankle.

Her clothes were bloody and ripped.

Her eyes were closed. Jason wasn't entirely sure she was breathing.

He forced every last piece of energy he had to his muscles, relying on adrenaline to force him to his feet.

Henry climbed to all fours, turning toward Jason and hissing. His eyeballs were succumbed by a complete bloody red, his hands wrapped around into claws, and its body curled up and tensing. It walked forward like an untamed beast, glaring at Julian, waiting for its turn to pounce.

The possessed body of Henry leapt forward, diving toward Julian, but Jason sent it on its side with a large swing of his fist, landing his knuckles in the side of the possessed man's face.

Jason managed to get himself back to his feet in time to thwack his asp around the back of Henry's head. Henry's body lay absently on the floor, eyelids flickering, losing consciousness.

Henry's body wriggled on the floor like a beast struggling to find its legs.

Jason swung his asp once more into Henry's head, knocking him out cold.

"We need to get him restrained, and now," Julian instructed. "We aren't going to do this without him still."

Jason withdrew his handcuffs and handed them to Julian.

"Use this," he instructed, then ran to Kaylee's side. He removed the restraints from the girl and held her dead weight in his arms, shaking her, willing her to come around.

The poor, wretched girl coughed, dribbling blood down her cheek. Then her coughing turned to desperate breaths, which turned to vacant wheezing.

She wasn't breathing.

He lay her down, wiping the trickling blood off her cheeks.

"No, come on..." he whispered, pleading with her to live, pleading even though it did nothing.

He thought back to his first aid training.

What should he do?

Don't panic.

That was the first thing. Don't panic.

Clear the airway. That was the next thing he remembered.

Taking a screwed-up piece of tissue from his pocket, he wiped away all the blood, patting her back to ensure everything came up.

He laid her firmly on her back and knelt beside her neck, opening her mouth.

He pinched the nostrils.

Took a deep breath.

Leant down, breathed oxygen into the little girl's lungs.

Looked at her chest.

It didn't rise.

The oxygen wasn't even going into her lungs.

What am I doing wrong?

He pinched her nose.

Why did I tell them to meet me at the station in an hour? How could I miss what that arsehole was doing to his daughter?

No time to think about that now.

Stop it.

Covering her mouth with his, pinching the nose, ensuring there was no way air could escape – he breathed out once more.

Her chest laid flat.

It did not rise.

The blood. She was choking up blood.

It must be clogging up her throat.

He resumed CPR.

He pumped her chest with his hands.

He gave her as much oxygen as he was able to give.

Again.

And again.

And again.

Nothing.

Absolutely nothing.

Jason turned and looked at Julian watching expectantly. He'd managed to handcuff Henry and find some rope that he was wrapping around him but he, just like Oscar and April, watched on helplessly, waiting to see if Kaylee lived or died.

"She's not breathing," Jason muttered, having to tell himself as much as the others.

As if with a protesting response, Kaylee spluttered a quick movement of her chest.

Jason's head shot back to her, watching her intently, the whole room holding a collective breath.

She spluttered some more.

Her chest rose.

He could feel her breath brushing against his cheek.

He turned back to the rest of the room.

"She needs to go to a hospital," Jason told them.

Julian looked from Jason, to Oscar and April.

"I'll take her," Oscar reluctantly decided. Out of everyone there he was evidently the most useless, and the one they could do without.

He stepped forward and began picking the girl up.

"No," Julian decided. Oscar turned back to him, bemused. "We need you, Oscar."

Oscar looked to April, then back to Julian. A flicker of happiness adorned his face, an emotion he tried to conceal; a young girl's life hung in the balance and this wasn't the time for him to be pleased that they needed him.

"Jason, could you?" Julian asked.

Jason nodded. "I'm going to need to call this in. How long do you need?"

"An hour."

"Okay."

Jason picked Kaylee up and swiftly took her away.

A CALM TRANQUILLITY DESCENDED OVER THE DINING TABLE OF the Kemple residence.

Henry, with his hands restrained in handcuffs through the back of his chair and an uncomfortable rope wrapped around his chest, opened his bloody eyes, surveying the scene with disgust.

The demon that dwelled within looked around itself, then grunted a sneer of amusement.

Julian sat directly opposite, with Oscar and April to his left and right. Sage sat on the table burning slowly, sending a small slither of smoke trailing into the air, surrounded by three lit candles. They held hands around the table, Oscar and April's hands crossing over Henry's body.

He leant his head back and guffawed. The demon's laugh rang out of Henry's helpless mouth, shaking the loose scabs poking off his face.

"You fucking idiots," it declared. "You're doing a séance, aren't you? Or is it a cleansing? Or a fucked-up kind of exorcism?"

"Please remember," Julian spoke to the other two, holding

eye contact with Henry's evil eyes. "To do exactly as I say, and do not break the circle."

Julian bowed his head and closed his eyes.

Henry grinned wildly, a sadistic curve smeared across his face. His laugh continued, high-pitched like a hyena, then low like a thunderous rumble in a distant jungle.

"Spirits, hear us," Julian began, slowly and calmly. "We have amongst us an unclean spirit."

"Hah!" Henry blurted out. "Unclean!"

"We need help casting this demon out of our brother's body."

Henry leant his head forward, turning to Oscar. "Hey," he whispered. "Hey, you."

Oscar opened his eyes, then turned away as Julian pulled on his arm, a prompt to ignore any taunts.

"Yo, Oscar, mate," Henry continued to whisper, as if he was talking to a naughty friend at the back of a class. "Wanna hear what I did to Kaylee?"

"If there are any spirits with us right now," Julian persisted, trying to ignore the demon's tease, "please help us cleanse this house of evil."

"Hey," Henry continued his sneaky whispers. "I practically broke her in two."

Oscar scrunched up his face, doing all he could to ignore the demon, refusing to give in to its sickening words.

"I fucked her in places you should never be fucked."

Oscar turned to Henry. He knew he shouldn't, he couldn't help it.

But he didn't see Henry sat beside him.

There, in its true form, was the demon Lilu. Its scarred body was decorated in a coat of armour, decorated like a war hero. But its face... its face sent shivers seizing up and down Oscar's chest. It was curved like that of a ravenous goat, twisted horns raising out of a contorted head, bloody fangs overlapping the edge of its mouth. Attached to its back were two large wings, almost as big as its body.

Then Oscar looked closer.

Its face… it wasn't just scrunched up out of a terrifying contortion of evil. It was upset. It was crying.

This thing was crying.

This gave Oscar an idea.

"You are pathetic," Oscar spoke.

"Oscar, what are you doing?" Julian demanded. They had forewarned Oscar not to interact with it and not to interrupt the process, yet there he was.

"A crying demon," Oscar continued. "How ridiculous."

"Oscar, what the hell are you–"

"Julian," April interjected, sensing that Oscar was onto something.

Julian calmed down and, despite being overcome by confusion, turned to Oscar and watched.

"Did you cry while you were raping her?" Oscar asked the demon, shocking himself momentarily at the words coming out of his mouth.

"How – how dare you!" the demon stuttered. "I will kill you!"

"Oh yeah, you gonna cry while you do that too?"

The demon roared, causing the candle flames to flicker manically, the table shaking.

Oscar shook his head, undeterred.

This demon's weakness was his weakness.

It was a loser. It got upset about pathetic, trivial things. It needed to be a man instead of some idiot weeping over a woman.

"Yeah, that would have been a lot more convincing if you weren't crying like a bitch."

"I – am not – crying!"

Oscar had never let anyone see him cry. He had taken medication to numb emotions so he didn't have to cry.

Because that would mean he cared.

He had never had a reason to care.

But now, looking around himself, he found his purpose. Julian, watching expectantly. April, astounded at his progress.

Beautiful, lovely, punky April.

Oscar was not like this sack-of-shit demon anymore.

And that was why he was going to win.

"You miss Ardat Lili, don't you?"

The demon's eyes narrowed, squinting into a devastated glare, fury depicted over its face. At least, it looked as if it was attempting fury. In truth, its menace grew less, its helpless eyes giving it away.

"You know what we did to Ardat Lili?"

The demon growled.

"We removed her from that body like a little bitch."

The demon released another deafening roar.

Oscar smiled. He was enjoying this.

"Oh yeah, go ahead and roar, that's so scary. At least I'm man enough to admit I'm a dipshit loser who can't get a girl. What are you?"

The table shook, vibrating uncontrollably. The sage quivered across it, the contents of the room trembling and shaking.

"Who do you think you are?" the demon screamed.

Oscar stood over Henry, looming over him like an uncontrollable shadow.

"Me?" Oscar stood, gyrating his finger at the demon, seeing its hold on Henry growing weaker. "I'm a loser who lives with his parents, works in a supermarket, needs meds to handle life, can't get a girl, gets looked down on by every person I see, gets intimidated easily, spends my days looking forward to my nightly masturbation session and is likely to never amount to shit!"

Oscar dropped his head closer to Henry's, until he was within inches, staring intensely into the demon's weakened eyes.

He felt the demon's tepid breath against his.

He didn't care.

He was not scared anymore.

This thing may have hooves.

It may be bloody.

It may be bigger, be evil, be far scarier than Oscar ever would be.

But it couldn't beat Oscar. Couldn't even mount a challenge.

Oscar had a gift.

He had friends.

There was a girl in the world willing to talk to him.

But, most of all, Oscar had grown something this crying-baby-demon didn't have.

A set of balls.

"So, you tell me," he spoke coolly and particularly, with an aggressive calmness. "Who's the real loser?"

The demon's final roar shook the house, causing glassware to fall off shelves and smash, photo frames to go sailing across the room, the table to fly into the far wall.

Then it all dropped.

Henry's body collapsed to the floor.

Oscar watched in awe as he saw the translucent figure of the demon rise into the air, out of Henry's mouth, then, with a scowl in Oscar's direction, dive hastily into the floor below.

Julian leapt forward, putting his hands on Henry's neck, feeling a pulse.

"He's alive," Julian observed, then glanced at his watch. "We need to go."

"But–"

"No, Oscar. You've done great, but the police will be here soon, let them deal with it."

Julian gathered up his things and, within minutes, was rushing out of the house.

Oscar and April followed.

And, as they did, her hand crept into his.

"Well done," she whispered. Then, with a cheeky grin, "Loser."

Three months later

4 3

Jason entered the interrogation room, taking his time. He glanced at Henry sitting there helplessly, hands restrained to the table, an unflattering prison outfit looking just as glum as his face.

Jason sat opposite him, undoing Henry's restraints and handing him a coffee. He leant back in his chair, sipping on his hot drink.

"How are you?" Jason asked.

Henry shook his head and snorted.

"How do you think?"

"What did your lawyers say?"

"They said I could possibly get away with temporary insanity. But they think it's unlikely."

Jason reluctantly nodded in agreement.

"Yes, it is. It's worth going for, but with the prolonged torture of Kaylee, and the death of…" Jason drifted off, seeing Henry's face flinch at the mention of his wife's suffering. "Out of curiosity, how much do you actually remember?"

Henry shrugged.

"It comes back in glimpses. Mostly in my dreams."

Jason took a sip of his coffee.

"The good news is that Kaylee is alive, and she's doing well. Doctors expect her to make a full recovery. I mean, physically, anyway."

Henry nodded, forcing a smile, telling himself this was good news.

"What about the Sensitives?" he asked, leaning forward.

"What about them?"

"Couldn't they testify? Tell people what really happened? If they were seen as experts, and they explained it, then surely…"

"And say what?" Jason asked.

A moment of silence passed as the question hung in the air.

"Unfortunately," Jason began, "you're not the first guy to come through here saying that voices made you do it."

Henry bowed his head. "So long as Kaylee is safe."

"I promise you, we will do all we can to make sure she goes to a good home, you can be sure of that."

Henry nodded.

I guess I'll have to settle with that.

"Thank you," he spoke, staring at a coffee stain on the floor. "I appreciate that."

"So, when are you going to take him to meet Derek?" April asked Julian. "I know he'd be dying to meet him."

Julian just smiled, keeping his answer to himself, watching Oscar across the hallway in the kitchen, in deep conversation on the phone.

"He always spoke about searching out other people like them," April insisted.

"You haven't even met him yet. Why would I take him?"

"Well, why not? He's evidently powerful, isn't he? Probably more so than he realises."

Julian didn't answer. He just stared intently at the young man having an animated discussion. It was true, Oscar was not the person they had first discovered. He had grown into his role, displaying confidence and gifts they could never have predicted.

Maybe it was worth putting more faith in him.

* * *

OSCAR FINISHED HIS PHONE CALL, placed his phone in his pocket and paused.

How great was this?

Something worth investing in. Something with purpose. Something that took him away from the monotony of his previous pointless existence.

He sauntered into the living room, glowing with the radiance of a happy smile.

"We have a poltergeist in Edinburgh," Oscar announced. "Or so they claim."

"Edinburgh?" April repeated, turning to Julian. "That's a hell of a trip."

"Is it worth investigating?" Julian asked.

Oscar paused.

Was it worth investigating?

Well, the woman sounded hysterical. Possibly a religious nutjob. A whacko desperate for attention.

But she was offering £3,000 for investigating.

"Yeah, I'd say so," Oscar decided.

"Well, Jason's just called," Julian pointed out, "says he has a job in Nottingham for a couple who keep hearing things in their attic. Wants us to take a look."

"Could we do it on the way?" Oscar offered.

"Road trip!" April declared. "And maybe we could pay your friend a visit on the way…"

"What friend?" Oscar quizzically inquired.

Julian just smiled knowingly. Oscar wondered who they were referring to, but didn't have a chance to ask. Julian stood, grabbed the car keys from the window-sill and chucked them in April's direction.

"Shotgun!" he declared.

And with that, they prepared their bags and left.

Julian leading the way.

April following behind, joking with Oscar.

Oscar, smiling.

Finally finding somewhere he belonged.

WOULD YOU LIKE TWO FREE BOOKS?

Get your free horror novella when you join Rick Wood's Reader's Group at **www.rickwoodwriter.com/sign-up**

I Do Not Belong

Death of the Honeymoon

Sean Mallon:

Book One – The Art of Murder

Book Two – Redemption of the Hopeless

The Edward King Series:

Book One – I Have the Sight

Book Two – Descendant of Hell

Book Three – An Exorcist Possessed

Book Four – Blood of Hope

Book Five – The World Ends Tonight

Non-Fiction

How to Write an Awesome Novel

Thrillers published as Ed Grace:

The Jay Sullivan Thriller Series

Assassin Down

Kill Them Quickly